Summer at Stewart Creek

written by
J. Arthur Moore

Omnibook Co. New York, New York

Printed in New York by:

OMNIBOOK CO.
99 Wall Street, Suite 118
New York, NY 10005
USA
+1-866-216-99652
www.omnibookcompany.com

portrait sketches by Diana Kingman
photo editing by Allen E. Miller Jr.

For e-book purchase: Kindle on Amazon, Barnes and Noble
Wholesale purchase: Ingram (615) 793-5000,
Baker & Taylor (800) 775-1800
Book purchase: Amazon.com, Barnes & Noble.com, www.jarthurmoore.com
and www.omnibookcompany.com/journeyintodarkness/

Omnibook titles may be purchased in bulk for educational, business,
fund-raising, or sales promotional use. For more information
please e-mail info@omnibookcompany.com

DEDICATION

Summer at Stewart Creek is dedicated in His love and in friendship to James, Paul, and Andy Wunderlich who helped to bring the story to life by becoming a part of the story through their images as the characters in the story. It is also dedicated to Brett and Adam Thomas and Jason Jones for whom the story was originally written as a remembrance of a special summer at Camp Good News on Cape Cod, Massachusetts, during the summer of 1979.

Brett

Adam

Jason

ARTWORK

All illustrative material – photographs, maps, drawings – are by the author, with one exception. The drawings of Brett, Adam, and Jason found on the dedication page, were contributed by a parent of one of the author's students, the year the manuscript was written. Cover photographs and portrait of Brett were taken with the "Tahoe", V&TRR locomotive #20, at the Pennsylvania Railroad Museum in Strasburg, Pennsylvania. The remaining photographs of the boys were taken at Hopewell Furnace National Historic Site near Elverson, Pennsylvania. The setting photographs were taken of the author's model railroad layout. .

L–R Wunderlich brothers Andy as Jason Johnston, Paul as Adam Tyler, and James as Brett Tompkins / these boys and their mother are currently a key part of the author's team in the presentation of Civil War living history programs sharing the history of the real boys who served in the opposing armies of the American Civil War.

https://www.jarthurmoore.com
https://www.facebook.com/Blakes-Story-623795801054538/

AUTHOR'S NOTE

Contrary to common practice, names which this author uses in the series of stories which take place along or are related to the Virginia and Truckee Railroad in West Virginia, do have meaning.

The setting itself grew out of the author's hobby of model railroading and is in part duplicated in miniature recreations. Photos from the model railroad are used throughout to provide images of the setting of the story. There is, however, a real railroad of the same name and period located in the state of Nevada near Virginia City.

Most of the names of places and characters are from real people and places in the author's experience as a middle grades school teacher, or from places and friends who have been a part of the author's life experiences. All have been chosen from good memories and are a way of saying, "I haven't forgotten you, though we haven't seen each other in years and may never meet again."

Often main characters are created for specific people and stories are dedicated to those individuals. Yet in a sense all the stories which are created as a part of the Virginia and Truckee series are dedicated to life's memories and the people who have been a part of those memories.

CONTENTS

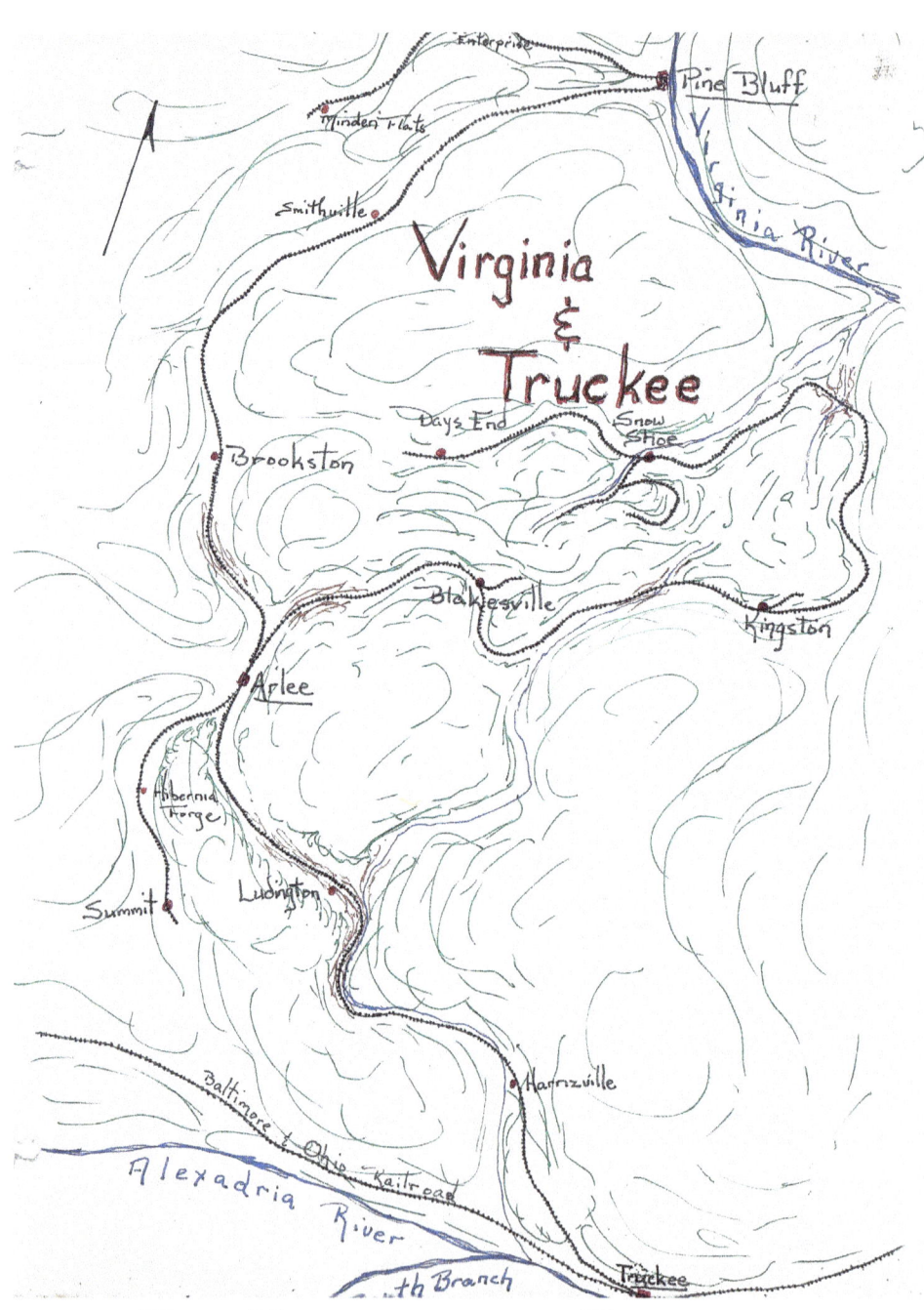

THE VIRGINIA AND TRUCKEE
RAILROAD (A MAP)

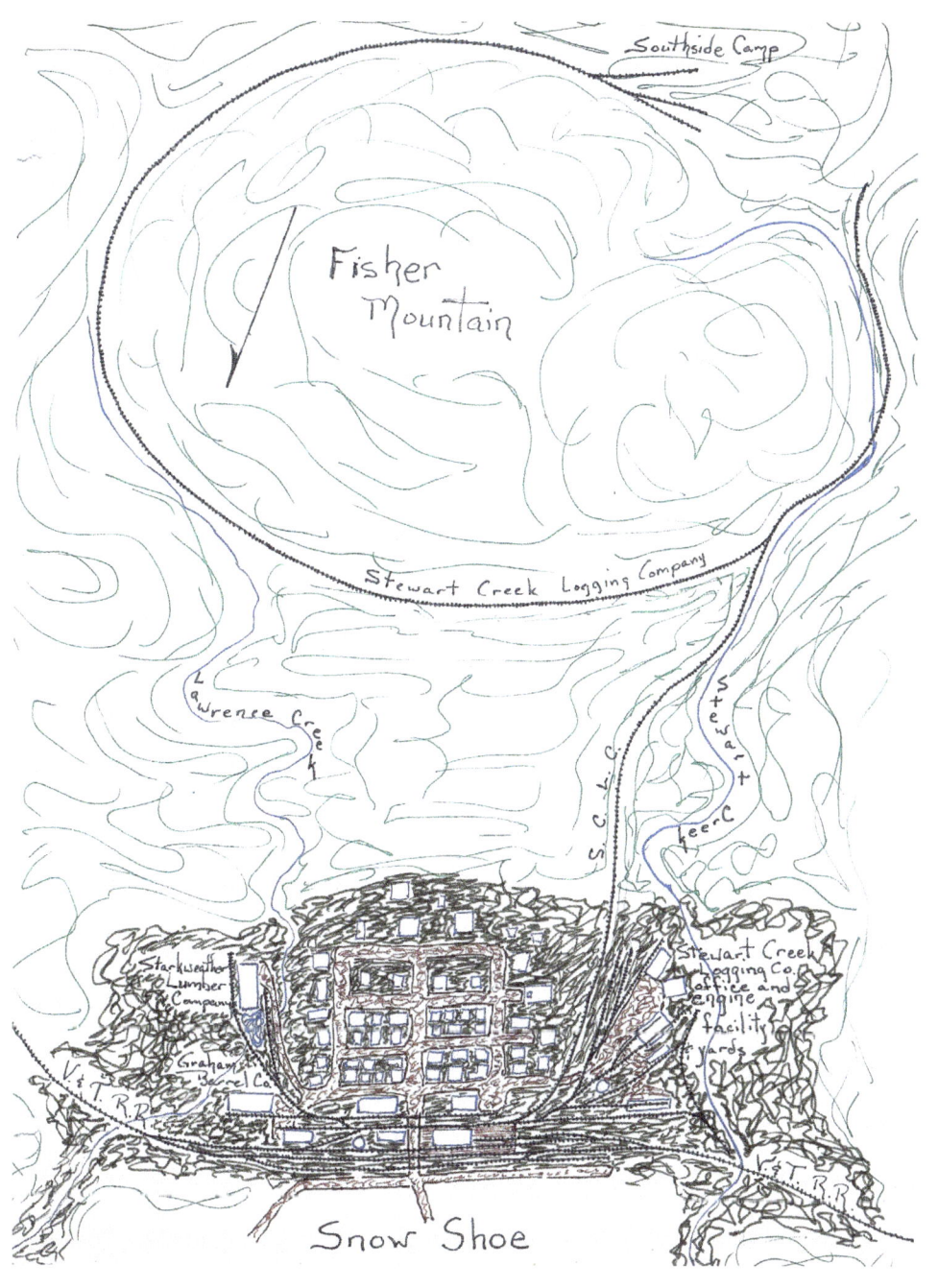

SNOW SHOE (A MAP)

BRETT TOMPKINS

ADAM TYLER

JASON JOHNSTON

OVERNIGHT IN ARLEE

The dark countryside flashed past outside the coach windows. Occasionally the light of a distant farmhouse could be seen. Darkness was coming on and Brett could see his reflection dimly in the window glass. The green plaid flannel shirt collar lay over his brown leather vest. His auburn brown hair, roughly cut, was slightly mussed up from his hat, which had been stowed on the overhead rack. The clear blue eyes appeared tired. Brett Tompkins had left from Baltimore the evening before. He remembered the last look at his mother, smiling and waving good-bye as tears streaked her face. The trip to Snow Shoe in the West Virginia mountains took more than two days and required transferring from the Baltimore and Ohio Railroad to the Virginia and Truckee Railroad at Truckee, West Virginia with another train transfer at Arlee. Brett had already made the change at Truckee and would arrive at Arlee in about an hour.

The boy leaned back, closed his eyes, and thought again of the events that had led up to this trip. His father's family had been in the logging business for four decades, but his father had been in banking in Baltimore, with no real interest in the logging company. Last summer, Grandfather Tompkins had visited and asked Teddy, Brett's father, for help. Grandpa's health was poor and he could no longer manage to operate the business. There was need of a family manager to operate the company, or it would be lost. Teddy was excited about the challenge and accepted. His wife, Elizabeth, would have no part of it. As things turned out, Teddy and Eli decided he could give it a try for a year. But she and Brett would remain in Baltimore. Brett's father left in September and took over the operation of the Stewart Creek Company at Snow Shoe in the West Virginia logging country.

Eli would not visit at Christmas or allow Brett to go. So his dad had come home. She did agree that after Brett turned eleven in the spring, he could go up to visit. So it was that in June of 1879, after school was out, Brett left for an unusual summer at Stewart Creek.

The engine's whistle cut in on the boy's thoughts. He looked out the window and saw lights ahead. As the train slowed, Brett saw the engine facility for Arlee outside the window with several engines sitting silent on the tracks, and one with smoke and steam rising from it to give it a ghostly appearance in the darkness. The brakes squealed sharply and the train eased to a stop at the Arlee station. A final rush of air and the brakes were locked in place. There followed a general commotion of voices and movement as a number of people got off the train. Brett took down his bags and put on his hat, then headed for the door with the rest of those who were getting off.

Once on the station platform, he walked away a short distance and turned to watch as the new passengers boarded. When the area had cleared, the conductor waved toward the engineer. The whistle sounded two long blasts. The bell began it's rhythmic ringing. A rush of air released the brakes with a clatter. A blast of steam started the drivers to turn slowly, and the train eased into forward motion. The light from the windows and the rumble of wheels faded into the distance as the train headed north toward Pine Bluff. The station area was quiet.

Brett sat down on a bench near a lamp and took out his father's letter from a pocket. He knew he was to spend the night at Arlee and take the morning train to Snow Shoe. He read again his father's instructions.

"When you arrive at Arlee, go to the Railroad Hotel, just across the street. Mrs. Johnston is the manager and she'll be expecting you..."

"Hi." Brett looked up into the squinting smile of a boy about his own age.

"Hi," Brett replied. "You shook me some."

"You must be Brett Tompkins," the boy said. "I'm Jason Johnston. My ma runs the hotel and said you'd be comin'." He brushed back his brown hair. "Come on. I'll take you over."

"Thanks. It's good to meet someone. The trip's been real lonely." The two boys picked up Brett's luggage and walked across to the hotel. The lighted building was a welcoming sight. Inside the lobby of the old wooden structure, several people were still checking in. Jason and Brett waited patiently while the last family finished checking in.

"Hi, Ma. I found him all right." He turned to Brett, "This is my ma, Mrs. Johnston. She runs the hotel. My pa owns it. But he also runs the Wells Fargo office and is over there just now."

"You must be tired and hungry, Brett," Mrs. Johnston offered. "Why don't you take him up to your room, Jason, so he can put his bags away. Then the two of you come down to the kitchen for somethin' to eat."

Jason led the way down the hall to the kitchen and up the back stairway. "We figured you could share my room tonight so your pa wouldn't have to pay for you a room. Besides, we could get a chance to talk, and I'd sure like the change. Guess you might, too."

Brett smiled. "Thanks. It'll be nice having a friend for a change." They put the bags on the floor just inside the door. In the distance a whistle sounded.

"The evening crew is moving cars around to be ready for the morning trains," Jason explained. "Your train was the last one through tonight. Things'll be quiet until the 4 AM southbound freight goes through." They headed back toward the kitchen. "Then it gets really busy working all the local traffic for the morning."

"Sounds like you live in a busy place. Our home in Baltimore is in a quiet part of town. Sometimes it gets awfully boring."

They returned to the kitchen. "Make yourself ta home, Brett. There's leftover chicken and potatoes which I'd kept aside for you and some cake and milk afterwards."

Jason watched as his new friend ate, asking and answering questions along the way. He discovered that his guest was older by a year, and a bit taller as well. His mother had cake and milk for both of them. Afterwards she excused Jason from helping clean up so he could show Brett around. The two of them retired to Jason's room.

From somewhere downstairs, a clock chimed nine o'clock. "That's my ma's clock in the sittin' room," commented Jason. "If you want, we can get to bed and lay awake and talk. As long as the lamp is out, Ma won't complain."

"Sounds fine." They changed into their night shirts and climbed into Jason's bed. "What's it like living in a hotel?" inquired Brett.

"It's pretty neat. Ya get to meet a lot of people. Most who stay here are pretty regular people and workers along the railroad. The richer people stay at the Grand Hotel over on Front Street. They miss out on the news. We know just about everythin' that goes on from Truckee to Pine Bluff and on over to Snow Shoe. My windows open on rail yards out back and the main line on the side."

An engine with a pair of boxcars rumbled past outside the window.

"Come look," Jason invited. "That's Tom Jennings and his crew in "Flanagan" Number twenty-eight. They're spotting cars on the siding for tomorrow morning's run to Summit. When they're finished, they'll bank the firebox and sleep in the caboose until things start to move in the morning."

"You sure know a lot about what goes on around here," remarked Brett.

"I ought to. I've lived here all my life. Someday I'll join the railroad and get to see some of the country. I've never really gone anywhere except to visit some relatives in Pine Bluff once."

The boys talked on into the night. Finally, in the middle of their conversation, Brett fell asleep. Jason turned over on his side and he too went sound asleep.

*   *   *

A screaming whistle, approaching quickly from some distant place, shocked Brett out of a peaceful slumber. At first he didn't know where he was or what was happening. He looked at the sleeping form beside him, then to the window nearby. It was dark outside. There was that noise again. The other boy turned in his sleep. The dim features of his face looked familiar. Then Brett remembered.

He crawled out of bed carefully so as not to disturb Jason. Stepping slowly, he moved to the window as the southbound freight rumbled past. Subconsciously he counted the cars as they clicked over the rail joints, sixteen in all. It was quiet again. Brett sat by the window awhile, then crept back to bed.

About an hour passed. Activity began at the yards and the noise of engines chugging about and of squealing metal drifted in the window. Brett lay awake listening. A growing sense of excitement churned inside. Today he would see his father. Until yesterday, the trip had been so dull and uneventful. But the time Brett had spent with Jason and the new friendship he had found had turned his stay in Arlee into an adventure of sorts, or maybe the beginning of a whole summer of adventure.

"You awake?" Jason spoke quietly. "Yea. Saw the freight go by at four. What's happening now?"

"The yard crews are gettin' the engines fired. They're puttin' on coal and puttin' in water. There'll be a lot o' action 'round here for the next several hours."

"How much can we see?" Brett inquired.

"I hafta help with chores 'til breakfast is cleaned up. Then we can go over to the station and watch."

The boys dressed, made up the bed, and went on down to the kitchen.

"Morn'n, Ma. Is Pa out back?"

"He's splittin' wood."

"Can I help?" asked Brett.

"Sure. Gatta fill the wood box and the water reservoir."

In the wood yard Hank Johnston was splitting cord wood. He was a tall sturdy man with long dark hair matted with sweat. The ax was buried in the chopping block as Mr. Johnston stopped working to meet Brett.

"Pa, this is Brett Tompkins. His pa runs Stewart Creek Company. This is my pa."

"Pleased to meet you, sir."

"Same here, Brett. Jason's ma tells me you two have become good friends. We're glad to have ya stayin' with us. Why don't you boys hurry up with the firewood and I'll take care of the water. That way you can have early breakfast and have some extra time together 'fore Brett's train leaves."

"Thanks, Pa."

"Thanks, Mr. Johnston. Come on. Show me where it goes."

The wood box was quickly filled. After breakfast Brett thanked the Johnstons for letting him stay with them. With his hat in his hand, he and Jason gathered his bags and went across to the station. There was lots of activity as the various trains came in. Jamming his hat on top of his head, Brett left his belongings on a bench while he watched.

The train from Summit came in. While the engine was in the yard taking on fuel and water and being turned around, Tom Jennings and his crew changed over the freight cars and spotted the train at the station. The engine returned from the yard and the Summit train moved into the pass track. Since Arlee was the center of transfer for the various branches, all morning trains had to meet to exchange passengers and freight cars. The train came in from Snow Shoe, dropped an empty baggage car, unloaded, had its engine turned, then moved onto the pass track with the train for Summit. Number twenty-eight moved the car to the yard.

At eight sharp the southbound coach from Pine Bluff and the northbound from Truckee arrived, one on either side of the station. Activity on the station platform was in general confusion as passengers got off or on and baggage and mail were exchanged. At 8:10, both trains pulled out of the station and activity slowed down as new arrivals were met and left or simply went on their own to take care of the private purposes for which each had come to Arlee. The train for Summit moved into the station, took on passengers, baggage, and mail, then left for the run back to Summit.

It was time to say good-bye. Number Twenty-One pulled out of the pass track into the station area. Brett picked up his bags.

"Wait," said Jason. "I want you ta meet someone. Come with me. Leave your things a minute."

"Where're we going?"

"To the engine." He hurried ahead. "Hi, Jay!"

The man in the cab waved. "How ya doin', Jason. Haven't seen ya lately." Soot marked the man's bearded face and clothes.

"Jay, I want ya to meet a real important friend o' mine." They stood under the engine's cab window. "This is Brett Tompkins."

"I shoulda knowd," the engineer interrupted. "His pa told me this mornin' I was pickin' him up."

"You know my dad?"

"Sure do. I work this branch regular and also work the "Scott" for the loggin' line. Better hurry on. I'm a minute late ta leavin'."

"See ya tomorrow," Jason called as they went back for Brett's things.

"So long, Jason. Be good till then." He pulled the whistle cord two long blasts while the fireman set the bell to ringing.

"I'm gonna miss ya, Brett." They stood by the coach steps.

"Me, too. It's been a really great stay. I feel as though I've known you for all my life. I sure hope I'll see you again."

"Sure do," said Jason. "I'll send a letter with Jay sometime."

Brett returned. "I'll let you know what it's like out there. Maybe my dad will let you visit if it's okay with your folks."

"Hope so."

"All aboard!" called the conductor. Brett dashed for the steps and the conductor helped him up as the wheels began to turn. The black smoke boiled from the stack as the pistons slowly churned. He was on his way again, on the final leg of his journey.

"Bye, Brett!" The wheels rumbled.

"Bye, Jason!" He shouted over the noise.

The boy watched from the car's platform as the station, his friend, then the town of Arlee slipped away behind. A sudden feeling of loneliness and great sadness swept over Brett as he turned to enter the coach. He'd never felt so close to a friend before and he missed Jason so much that it hurt. Yet he hadn't even known him one full day.

At the station, Jason stood on the platform staring down the empty track watching the last wisp of smoke drift away on the morning breeze. He felt strangely empty inside. Wiping aside quiet tears, he turned away and started back toward home. Breakfast dishes would be waiting.

ARRIVAL IN SNOW SHOE

The train moved slowly and noisily through the rugged mountain country. North of Arlee it switched off the main line, passed through Guyer's Cut and into the Ramsey Hills. Opening into a small valley, the train slowed as it approached Blakesville.

Dan Seegers, a man in his thirties with thinning blond hair, was the conductor on the train. He glanced up from his paperwork, took off his glasses, and watched the boy sitting across the aisle. The boy had been watching the countryside pass by the window. Yet he seemed very quiet.

"You're Teddy's boy, aren't ya," Dan stated.

Brett turned toward the voice. "Yes, sir," he replied.

"Had a good trip?"

"It's okay." He looked back out the window. "The sign says this is Blakesville. Sure is small."

Dan offered information. "We stop mainly for mail. Sometimes there are passengers, but that's usually on the weekend. Blakesville is only here because of a coal mine, a gristmill, and a freight house for farm goods." The train squealed to a halt. "Excuse me, Brett. I'll be right back."

Dan left the coach. Watching through the window, Brett saw him step down to the wooden station platform and walk toward the head of the train. After losing sight of the conductor, the boy glanced over at the station area. Beyond was a track ending at a mill building and a warehouse. Toward the north a line wound off into the hills.

The conductor came back toward the car. He caught Brett's attention and motioned him to get off the train. The boy wondered at the reason for this as he descended the steps.

"Jay wants ya up front," Dan informed. Brett walked quickly toward the engine.

"Brett," Jay called. "Must be boring back there. How'd ya like to ride up here a while?"

"Sure!" Brett exclaimed, breaking into a smile and reaching for Jay's outstretched arm. Jay grasped Brett's wrist as the boy gripped with both hands, and hoisted him up into the engine cab.

"Set here," the fireman, Scot O'Donnell, motioned to a seat by the window.

"All aboard," conductor Seegers called. Jay jerked the whistle cord two long blasts as Scot set the bell to ringing. The engineer eased the throttle lever forward. Steam surged into the pistons and the engine slowly eased forward. Brett watched out the window as steam rolled up from the pistons and black smoke billowed from the stack. He felt the vibrations of the engine in his body as it came to life in majestic motion. The thrill of it tingled down his back.

"Betcha it's the first you've been in an engine's cab," Jay spoke. "Probably won't be the last either." He smiled toward the boy.

"Yes, sir!" was all Brett could manage.

Scot shoveled on coal and checked the gauges.

"Connell's Crossing ahead," Jay announced. "Grab the cord up there," Jay pointed. Brett did so. The engineer wrapped his sooty hand around Brett's and pulled -- two long wailing calls, a short blast, and another long wail which seemed to hang on the air.

It echoed back over the hills as the engine rumbled across a rutted mountain road. Nobody in sight.

"That sounds neat!" the boy grinned.

"Next time I'll tell ya when. Then you do it," Jay instructed.

Twenty minutes later Scot said they were approaching Kingston. Brett watched the town glide closer. Jay motioned and the boy sounded the whistle. Somehow it didn't have quite the same character as when Jay had helped him.

Judging from empty coal cars, Kingston had a coal mine, too. Stock pens and ramps suggested that livestock were shipped from here as well. The train had hardly stopped when Dan gave the signal to move on.

"Show Shoe is next," announced Jay. Brett began asking questions as they rumbled toward the end of the journey. Jay and Scot took turns explaining the engine's workings and the landmarks along the route.

The train was approaching a bend when Jay pulled back on the throttle and eased to a slow crawl. He jerked the whistle cord once as they rounded the bend. Brett was surprised to see a boy of about eighteen appear from nowhere along the brush, reach for a grab iron, and haul himself into the cab. The engine picked up speed.

"How's the track ahead, Jamie?" Scot asked.

"Fine, all the way. Some loose spikes on Chamber's Crossing should be set by this afternoon's crew when they're down."

"Thanks," Jay responded. "I want ya to meet Mr. Tompkin's son, Brett. This here's Jamie Rhodes, Brett. He walks the tracks down from Snow Shoe every mornin' to meet us before Chamber's Crossing. He checks to see if the bridge is safe mostly, and looks for any other problems along the way."

The four of them talked about the business of the day ahead and matters of curiosity to Brett. The train rumbled across Chamber's Crossing, which carried the tracks across a creek in a cut about fifty feet deep. The engine's progress echoed on through wooded mountainsides.

The train rounded one last bend, then slowed for a switch. Jamie jumped down, ran ahead, and threw the switch. Jay eased the train through, then waited for Jamie to close the switch back and get aboard. Watching ahead, Brett saw that the train had moved off the main and onto a passing track. The trees opened up and revealed a bustling town nestled into a mountain hollow.

Snow Shoe's population was somewhere between six hundred and a thousand. It depended on the day of the week and the season of the year. The town was a logging town, built around the operations of the Stewart Creek Logging Company and related industries. At the west end of the town sprawled the logging company yards and facilities. The lumber mill, owned by William Starkweather, and the barrel works owned by Harold Graham, dominated the east end of town. The businesses, stores and shops followed Railroad Avenue, the main thoroughfare between these industries. North and south of the tracks were company houses, and tucked along the west edge of town, Reverend Jesse Moore's Methodist Church and a few private homes. Snow Shoe's station was tucked between the passing tracks off the main. The building was a relatively new wooden structure painted the standard yellow used on the majority of the railroad's structures. Dark brown door and window frames, and trim work added contrast to the building's appearance.

Few people waited on the platform for the approaching train. Brett could easily find his father, a short man whose skin had been tanned by months of working outdoors. He remembered how he had been surprised by the change in his father at Christmas. Once a pale looking man with solid brown hair, he had become weathered looking with sun-bleached hair, had gained in muscular strength and looked so distinguished and healthy. Brett loved his father dearly and had missed him greatly this past winter.

Scot spoke, "Brett, give the whistle one long and a short."

Brett let out a long wail and a short toot while the fireman set the bell to an even ringing. Jay eased back on the throttle and Number Twenty-One began to slow. The brakes screeched harshly. The train rolled to a gentle stop with the coach steps centered on the station building.

"Thanks, Jay. Thanks, Scot. This has been a really great ride." Brett reached out and shook their hands. A smile of joy and excitement lit his face. The two surprised men responded with firm handshakes. "See you later." He turned to climb down.

"Be careful gettin' down," Scot offered.

Brett backed down to the end of the wooden platform. His father spotted him.

"Dad! Dad!" He ran into strong outstretched arms in a loving hug. He squeezed his father tightly in return.

"Brett, it's so good to see you! God, how I've missed you and your mom!"

"I've missed you, too."

His father released his grip and held his son at arm's length. "How's your mom?"

"She's fine. She's not happy about being home alone. But she's goin' to Grandmom's for a few weeks."

Dan Seegers walked over from the coaches. "You have a good trip, Brett?"

"Great!"

"Your things are on the bench by the station door."

"Thanks," Mr. Tompkins said.

"Thanks, Dan." Brett offered his hand. "Thanks for being so kind."

The conductor shook the boy's hand. "We'll ride together again. Take care." He turned and walked back to the train.

"Come on, son. Let's get your things and I'll show you where we live."

They walked over to the bench. Brett grabbed the leather suitcase. His father picked up the carpet bag. They turned toward Main Street, which passed the end of the station platform. Small groups of people stood talking near the street and a Wells Fargo wagon was loading up packages and boxes that had been unloaded from the baggage car. Leaving the station activity behind, Brett and his father turned up Main Street. The sun shown warmly in a clear wispy-clouded sky and the streets of Snow Shoe bustled with mid-morning activity. It was hard to believe that only two and a half days had passed since Brett had said good-bye to his mom on Monday over three hundred miles away. It seemed so long ago.

"How was your trip?" his father asked.

"At first, very lonely. But it's been so great since yesterday. I really enjoyed meeting Jason in Arlee. And the crew on the train was so friendly."

"Who's Jason?"

"His mom runs the hotel."

At the corner of Railroad Avenue, they paused while a wagon went by.

"I've been living with the Tyler family on the south edge of town. That's three blocks from here. Mr. Tyler is a section foreman with the logging company. He has a son named Adam who's about a year older than you. I think you'll like him. Adam is a really outgoing kid, very easy to get along with. Their family has lived in this area for many years. So he knows his way around these parts as well as everyone."

The two of them walked the three blocks to Cedar Avenue. The Tyler residence was on a small farm of several acres and included most of the block on the south side between Main Street and Jeffers Street. Mrs. Tyler was sweeping the front porch as Mr. Tompkins and his son arrived. The house was a two story white frame structure with a porch across the front and along one side. A red barn and some out buildings were in the back.

"Hi, Janet," Mr. Tompkins waved as they approached the walk.

"Hi, Teddy. And this must be Brett. Its so good to have you." She set her broom against the railing and reached for his suitcase.

"I'll take this in. You must be hungry. I've soup on the stove and some sandwiches in the ice box. Come eat before you unpack."

They went into the front hall. Brett could smell the soup. Chicken, he thought. The house was very neat within. A center hall ran front to back. A parlor opened off the right of the front door and a large living room off the left. An open staircase led up to the second floor. At the back of the hall a bedroom was to the right and a dining room to the left. The kitchen was straight ahead. Brett's things were left in the hall at the foot of the stairs.

After lunch, Mrs. Tyler showed Brett to his room. He spent the rest of the afternoon settling in and telling his father the news from home and the experiences of his trip from Baltimore. His father told him about the town of Snow Shoe and some of what he had been doing during the past winter. At Brett's request, he found some paper and envelopes so Brett could write letters to his mother and to Jason. They would go out on tomorrow's morning train. The five o'clock whistles blew at the lumber mill and the logging company yard. Mr. Tyler would be home soon. His son would be with him and Brett would meet them both at dinner.

A Day with Adam

After dinner Brett helped Adam clear the table. Dirty dishes and left overs were taken to the kitchen where Adam's mother was putting the food away and washing. The boys did the drying and put the dishes away. Their fathers had retired to the living room to go over matters of business.

Adam was slightly taller than Brett. At thirteen he was tanned from being outdoors. His brown hair was cut close and lay neatly without combing. He had been telling Brett about life in a logging town and joking about a banking man running the business. The younger boy knew his new friend wasn't serious, only trying to be friendly and make him laugh. Adam had spent the day on the mountain with his father, not because he had too, but because he liked to be with him and enjoyed the adventure. Tomorrow he would stay home and the two of them would explore the town together while their fathers were at work.

At nine-thirty the boys were sent to bed. Adam's room was in the front of the house and Brett's was next door. Brett's father's room was across the hall from Adam's and also overlooked the front yard. Adam showed Brett his room and the collection of railroad and company paraphernalia he'd collected over the years. Among other things, he had tie plates, spikes, a boiler plate from an engine the company had scrapped, a lantern, and old timetables and way bills. The boys walked back to Brett's room.

"Ya wanta get up early and help me with my chores?" Adam asked.

"Sure."

"Okay. See ya then. Good night." Adam left the room.

Brett could hear him next door as he opened and closed his closet door and changed for bed. He closed his door and walked over to the back window. Looking out at the silhouette of the mountain under the clear starlit sky, the boy wondered at what adventure might be found on that mountain. Brett changed into his night shirt, blew out the lamp, and climbed between the sheets. Downstairs he could hear the quiet voices of the grownups. Soon he was asleep.

*　　*　　*

Adam's chores included feeding the livestock, milking the family cow, and carrying in firewood for the wood box by the kitchen stove. After seven o'clock breakfast, the men left for the company yards and Mrs. Tyler began gathering the dirty clothes for the Thursday washing. Adam and Brett left the house and walked east on Cedar to where it ended at the corner with Washington Street. Washington was a residential street, lined mostly with company houses belonging to the Starkweather Lumber Company. Cutting through back yards, they came to the lumber company. Activity was just beginning on the cars loaded with logs parked on the mill track. Adam led the way to the office at the end of the mill drive.

The grey-haired man looked up from the papers on his desk as the boys entered. "Mornin', Adam. Who's your friend?"

"Hi, Mr. Starkweather. This is Brett Tompkins. His father runs the logging company."

"Pleased ta meet ya, Brett." He stood and shook hands.

"Good morning, sir." Brett looked around at the desks, file cabinets, and boards of papers hanging on the walls. "Looks like a busy place."

"We ship a lot of lumber, son, at least three carloads a day."

"Is it okay if I show Brett around?" asked Adam.

"You know ta be careful."

"Thank ya, sir."

Mr. Starkweather returned to his paperwork as the boys left the office. They entered the main building. The air was already thick with sawdust and the scream of the saws ripping through logs. The boys were careful to stay out of the way of the operators as they moved around to watch logs brought up the runway, squared, then cut into boards. The boards were stacked on horse-drawn dolly carts and hauled to the yards to dry. Outside, boards from stacks of dried lumber were being loaded into boxcars. Adam explained that the ten cars of logs would be emptied and milled by noon and ten more would be brought down before lunch for the afternoon work. The empties would go up the mountain for another load. At the end of the afternoon there would be ten more loaded cars in place for tomorrow's operation. The loaded boxcars would be taken out during the afternoon for the morning freight run. Yesterday's loaded cars were already in the station yard being made up with the rest of the freight traffic.

The boys walked the tracks toward the station yard. "Bet I can walk a rail further than you," challenged Adam. Each balanced on a rail and at Adam's signal began walking carefully along the top edge. Brett swayed, then caught himself. A few steps further, his foot slipped and he fell on the gravel ballast. Adam jumped across the rail and helped him up.

"You okay?" he asked.

Brett stood up and brushed off the dirt. "Sure," he replied cheerfully. "Just need a bit more practice." He stepped back up on the rail's edge and walked along carefully for several yards before returning to the ties for better footing.

"That's the barrel company," Adam explained, pointing to a large wooden building to their right. They watched as engine Number Three backed into the siding pushing a pair of empty boxcars. It uncoupled and steamed forward out of the siding. They left the tracks and walked out onto the end of Railroad Avenue.

The first structure out of the mill area was the fire company. The doors stood open revealing two steam pumpers of polished brass and varnished red woodwork. Two elderly gentlemen sat in front of the building engrossed in a game of checkers. One white-whiskered grandfather glanced up.

"Mornin', Adam." He went back to his game.

"Mornin', Mr. Westly." Adam explained to Brett as they strolled on up the street, "The firehouse is usually pretty empty except when fire hazards are high. Then a crew is always ready and sometimes the horses are even hitched and ready to go. That'll probably be later in the summer when it hasn't rained for a long time."

The boys spent the morning on Railroad Avenue exploring the stores and businesses, and meeting people to whom Adam introduced Brett. They visited with Nathan Hall at the gun shop, watched Alex Hollis give haircuts, and checked out the merchandise in Harvey Jenkins' general store. Van Allen's Saddle and Harness Goods was explored from front to back. Brief stops were made at the Railroad Hotel and the sheriff's office. Brett was fascinated by the typesetting and press operation at the Herald. The proprietor, Evan Clanton, was a heavy set, grey-haired gentleman in his sixties. He was alert to every bit of news and history in the area for the past forty years and enjoyed showing the boys around and answering Brett's questions. He and Adam were old friends from as far back as Adam could remember. Adam worked part time for the Herald, and so he showed Brett some of the type setting operation.

It was late morning when they reached the livery stable. Henry Adams was busy at the forge fitting a new rim to a wagon wheel. Just beyond, the road led across the tracks of the logging company on into the company yard. A shrill whistle shrieked from up toward the mountain, and it's call echoed back from the trees.

"Come on!" Adam shouted. "That's the mornin' load comin' down from South Camp." He led off toward the tracks at a run with Brett close behind. They reached the rails and watched up toward the mountain as the plume of smoke marked the train's progress down the valley. There was a movement at the bend ahead. Brett could make out a carload of logs coming toward him. Soon he could distinguish the ten loaded log cars with the engine behind, backing slowly toward the crossing. The whistle blew for the crossing as the boys stepped back a safe distance. It rumbled slowly past, stopped for the switch, then continued on toward the mill.

"Time for lunch," Adam announced after the train was gone from sight. "Ma'll be lookin' for us."

They returned to the house by way of Jeffers Street, pausing long enough for Brett to take a look at the church. It was a white wooden structure with a tall pointed belfry which could be seen from almost anywhere in town.

*   *   *

The first week passed quietly. Brett received a letter from his mother telling how she missed him and giving the news from home. Obviously she hadn't received his when she wrote. It was dated the same day he had written to her. Jason wrote an answer to Brett's letter to him and said he hoped to visit. He was keeping himself busy around the hotel and went fishing some.

On Thursday evening of the second week, Mr. Tompkins told Brett that he could spend Friday with him on the mountain. That night as he prepared for bed, the boy looked out at the mountain as he'd done every night, and knew he'd finally see for himself what was up there.

ACCIDENT AT SOUTH CAMP

The tracks glistened with the early morning dew. At eight in the morning, the sun was already well above the mountain. Activity was under way in the yard as Brett and his father and Mr. Tyler walked toward the office.

Adam would be working with Evan Clanton for the day. The Herald went to press on Fridays for distribution throughout the area served by the Virginia and Truckee. Adam's job was to deliver the local papers and to see that the bundles for shipping were loaded on the baggage car.

Engine Number Two, the "Scott", had already been fired up and was waiting just outside the engine house while she built up steam. Smoke drifted lazily from the stack. Steam from the morning dew heating on the boiler, wrapped her in a fog-like blanket.

"See you two on the train," Mr. Tyler spoke. "I'll be seein' to the supplies with Dave and Buddy."

"Thanks, Bill. We'll check in at the office and pick up the mail." Mr. Tompkins and Brett turned toward the office building beside the engine house.

"Pa," Brett had begun to talk like the locals. "Jay once said he ran the "Scott" for the company. How can he do that and run Number Twenty-One for the V & T?"

"He takes the morning coach to Arlee and back and works the "Scott" in the afternoon. This being Friday, there'll be an extra evening train because most of the men leave the mountain on the weekend. Some live along the line. Others go off for a good time. Jay'll stay over in Arlee with the Johnstons and bring the train back tomorrow."

They entered the office. Work here was already under way. Brett had visited several times already. He knew that several people worked out of this office. Steven Jeffers, the maintenance boss, was busy checking a work order for repairs on two flatcars. Milton Lawrence did most of his work from this room. He handled orders and record keeping as well as the job of paymaster.

At present he was closing the mail bags, which were to go up with the train to South Camp. The V & T stationmaster, Robert Coates, was in and out daily to coordinate equipment servicing and maintenance since the railroad contracted all work on this branch to the Stewart Creek facility.

Brett looked around while his father went through the paperwork checking the day's work schedule and verifying the payroll. The old photographs hanging on the wall with the company map had caught his attention once before. He stopped again to study them.

"This man standing by the engine sure looks like Grandpa," the boy observed.

"It is your grandfather, son, many years ago when he first ran this company."

"Who's the boy with him?"

Teddy walked over to look again at an old memory. "That's me when I was your age. We lived here most of my childhood. The family property is just down from Tyler's where the Stephenson family lives."

"Pa, why did you leave?"

"I'll tell you on the way up the mountain." The "Scott's" whistle sounded. "The train's made up and ready to move."

"Mail's ready," Mr. Lawrence announced.

"Thanks, Milt. We'll see you tonight." He handed one of the bags to Brett as they left the office.

Outside, the engine was standing on the maintenance track. Its consist was made up of the company caboose followed by ten empty flats. The engine crew was busy in the cab. Two other men were standing beside the last flatcar. Mr. Tyler waited in the open freight door of the caboose.

The engineer leaned out the window. "Whenever you're ready, Ted."

"Let 'er go, Bob." Mr. Tompkins instructed. He handed the mail to Mr. Tyler who then rolled the door closed. The crew men climbed aboard the flat as Brett and his father mounted the steps to the caboose. Three short blasts of the whistle were followed by the slow churning of the pistons as the train began to ease backwards out of the siding. Brett watched the move from the platform. His father went in to review work orders with Mr. Tyler. One of the crew men jumped down as the train eased through the switch. When the "Scott" had cleared, he threw the switch to the company's main track, waited for the train to roll by, then jumped back on as the flat passed. The train chugged slowly up the valley following the bank of Stewart Creek.

Brett went into the caboose and sat down at the table to listen as his father recalled some of the events of his childhood. Mr. Tyler excused himself and walked out to the platform to watch the track for maintenance needs.

Theodore James Tompkins had been born and raised in Snow Shoe. He was the youngest of three children, and the only son of James and Ida Tompkins. Back then the settlement was a cluster of small homes, bunk cars, and tents. He had seen the change as the company houses replaced bunk cars and tents, and the businesses came and built. As the company profits grew and necessary facilities were completed, the family was able to build a nice home. When Teddy was older, his father began to worry about his education. The family moved to Baltimore, where most of the relatives lived, when Teddy was fourteen. His father continued to live part time in the house at Snow Shoe until ten years ago. The house was leased out and James Tompkins ran the business from Baltimore, with monthly trips to Snow Shoe. The direct supervision of operations was turned over to an elderly man named Ira Hurley. He had done a fine job until his death a year ago.

The train slowed, then stopped. "We're at the switchback," Mr. Tompkins explained. "How'd you like to ride the rest of the way in the "Scott"?"

"Yes, sir!"

Brett and his father scrambled down the steps as the train started to drift back. It stopped again as the fireman noticed them on the ground.

"We'll be up front, Bill," Brett's father informed. They hurried into the engine cab as the engineer moved the train backwards across the switch.

"Thanks, Bob," said Mr. Tompkins. "I'd like you to meet my son, Brett. Brett, this is Mr. Leary, the engineer, and Mr. Bond, the fireman."

Bob Leary was a chunky, square-faced man. Brett judged him in his fifties. Stewart Bond was maybe ten years younger, somewhat taller, and of lighter build.

Mr. Tompkins indicated for Brett to sit on the fireman's box. He in turn leaned up against the side of the box. Brett watched out the front. The cab door down the boiler walkway was open and gave a good view as the switch receded from sight. The train backed upgrade following the contour of the mountain. There was little conversation as Mr. Bond worked the fire and Mr. Leary kept a steady eye on the track. Mr. Tompkins watched the fireman's side of the track. The trip from the switchback to the main camp was just short of three miles. Periodically there were signs of where earlier camps had been -- large clearings where the trees had been harvested and new growth was well under way, and ties from which rails had been removed.

It was mid morning when the train rolled into the empty siding at South Camp. The camp was the busiest place Brett had seen since his arrival at Snow Shoe. Teamster crews were dragging logs in with horse teams and leaving them beside the flats left the day before. A steam crane crew loaded them on the cars as the teamsters left for another drag. A third track was occupied by the bunk cars where the men lived during the week. At the end of that track was the cook tent. Smoke drifted from the cook stove as the cook worked preparing noon meal. Beyond that was the corral where the horses were kept when not working. The ring of axes and saws echoed from the hillsides as other crews felled trees and cleaned off their branches. A periodic call of "timber!" followed by a crash announced the drop of another tree. Eight flatcars had full loads and the last two were nearly complete.

The fireman banked the fire. Bob set the brakes. They excused themselves and headed for the mess tent as Brett and his father walked to the caboose.

"Dave. Bud." Mr. Tompkins called to the men who had ridden up on the flatcar. "Let's get these supplies over to Horace. Brett, help me pass them down."

"I'll be checkin' on the work. See ya shortly, Ted." Mr. Tyler walked off toward the loading operation.

The boy and his father climbed aboard and opened the caboose freight door. The boxes of food supplies were passed down to the crewmen who carried them over to the mess tent. It took three trips to complete the job. The mailbags and other boxes of replacement tools and materials were unloaded and put into a storage tent. The four of them then joined the engine crew in the mess tent.

Mr. Tompkins introduced his son to a short, shaggy-bearded man who was pouring coffee for them.

"Howdy." Horace's greeting was short and crisp. He limped back to the stove.

"Don't let his gruffness worry you," offered Stewart. "He's like that with everyone."

"Thanks." Brett turned to his father. "Is this coffee for me, too?"

"If you want, son. I know you're not used to it, but you're allowed to drink it."

The other section foreman came in.

"Mornin', Teddy."

"Morning, Dick. How's progress?" He listened to the report on the morning's work. "Brett, Mr. Cantrell and I are going over to check in the tools and materials and review the schedule. Make yourself at home. I'll be back shortly."

Brett left the men at the table and walked over to the cook tent.

Horace was cutting vegetables for the pot. "Mr. Leeds, is there anything I can do to help?"

"What!" Horace dropped the knife on the ground. "You're the boss man's kid." He turned to Brett in surprise.

"Does that matter?" Brett wondered.

"Naw, I guess not. Ya kin move them tin plates and that box o' forks over ta the tables." He watched in amazement as Brett did as instructed. A frown of approval creased his face as he picked up the knife, wiped it on his apron, and continued cutting.

Brett busied himself with odd jobs in the kitchen until his father returned.

"I hope he wasn't in the way," Mr. Tompkins apologized.

"Humph! No trouble," came the short reply.

"Comeon, Son, I'll show you around."

They spent the rest of the morning exploring the camp. Brett looked into the bunk cars. He watched the loading operation and even tried his hand at securing a guide rope to one of the logs. They looked over the corral and harness shed. The boy caressed the neck and ran his fingers through the mane of a sturdy brown mare. She nibbled on some hay he fed her. The "Scott's" whistle announced noon meal and the crews came in to eat.

The engine then picked up the loaded flats, left the empties in their place, and left the caboose on the empty siding. The train left and headed back down the mountain.

Some eight dozen men drifted in from the hillsides. The horses were tied along the fence rail to rest. The section foremen passed out the mail which Mr. Tompkins had given them earlier. After a brief quiet spell while the men were reading their mail, the huge mess tent was loud with conversation and stories. Brett was introduced and got to meet several of the men. He sat between his father and Mr. Tyler. The air became mixed with the smells of stew and coffee, sweat and wood chips, and the sound of boisterous talk. The boy liked it and resolved to ask his father if he could find some kind of job so he could work in the camp at least part time.

After the noon break, Mr. Tompkins and his section foremen had a brief meeting; then they went off to direct afternoon operations. A work crew quickly put end stops on each of the empty flatcars converting them for pulpwood. The first part of the afternoon would be spent putting on a load of pulpwood cut from the week's worth of branches from the trees cut throughout the week for the mill. These would ship out to the paper mill at Brookston on the Monday freight run. The "Scott" would return in mid-afternoon for a quick change, and would be back again for the last load for the saw mill.

Mr. Tompkins was busy during the first hour of afternoon work. Brett occupied himself by wandering around the camp, stopping to watch the loading for awhile and again to pet the mare. His father found him back at the mess tent talking with Horace. Brett did most of the talking. Horace said very little.

"Brett, we're going up on the slope to where Mr. Tyler's section is logging. You'll get to see how the operation works."

The first part of the hill was barren except for the stumps of fallen trees. Another nearby area which had been cut months ago was already in new growth as the smaller trees and newly planted seedlings had benefited from the extra sunlight. They entered the active work area.

"Teddy! Watch out!" The air exploded with a loud crack as a nearby tree trunk snapped.

Brett heard the crashing of shattering wood rushing toward him. Looking up, he saw a shadow race across the sky. He felt himself pushed down. Then suddenly everything went black.

Several men came running. "Tom, get Bill Tyler!"

"On the way!"

"Lyle, you and Harry cut the top. Al, get Horace and bring a wagon. Jamie, you and Simon hitch your team to the trunk and steady it while we cut from under this side."

They worked frantically to cut the limbs that pinned Mr. Tompkins and his son to the ground. Mr. Tompkins started to move.

"Hold still, Teddy. We're cuttin' ya out!" the crew leader called.

"Brett!" his father called. "Brett! Sean, can you see my son! Is he all right?"

"Hold a minute. I'm almost in."

Brett could hear voices and the sawing. He felt a heavy pressure pushing his body into the ground. He realized there was pain. He felt it in his head and in his chest. At first everything was fuzzy and far away. Suddenly all was crystal clear and the pain cut through him sharply.

"Pa! It hurts!" he screamed.

"I'm right here, Son. Don't try to move!"

"Brett, this is Sean. We'll have ya free in a few minutes. Jest don't move."

The boy wanted to cry. He looked for his father. Bill Tyler came running across the hill. "My God! What happened?" he exclaimed.

"The boy and his father are pinned," one of the men answered.

Brett realized his father must be hurt too. Sudden concern for his father tended to dull his own pain some. The boy relaxed a bit. "Pa, you hurt?" He winced with pain. The saws ripped clear and he felt the pressure released from his body. The shift caused new pain and he screamed sharply.

"Hang on, Brett. Bill knows what he's doing." Brett felt something hot and sticky on his face. He felt it running down his neck and touched it with his hand. Blood. Several hands reached for him and held him so he couldn't move. Pain and fear were temporarily calmed knowing someone was there.

"Where does it hurt?" Mr. Tyler asked.

"My head and inside."

"How about your back or neck?"

"No!" The boy gritted his teeth.

He felt hands run down his arms and legs.

"Can you feel this?"

"Uh huh."

"Any pain in your arms or legs?"

"No."

A wagon rumbled up.

"Horace, throw me some bandages and see ta Teddy," Mr. Tyler instructed.

The sawing to clear the opening had stopped completely. The men stood by to help. They spoke quietly and moved on signal knowing what was to be done. Sean took the bandages and folded a cloth to cover a gash on Brett's head and bandaged it in place. Mr. Tyler pulled up the boy's torn shirt and ran experienced fingers up his back and traced his ribs.

"Ow!" Brett cried.

"Easy, boy. You've a couple cracked bones here," the foreman explained. "We're goin' ta move ya slowly. Let us do the work."

Carefully they moved the boy out into the open. Mr. Tyler wrapped a tight bandage around Brett's chest, then eased him onto his back. He explored his abdomen carefully for any swelling.

"Any pain down here?"

"Uh uh," the boy replied. "Where's Pa?"

"I'm over here, Son. Horace is doing a fine job. I'll get to you in a minute."

"No such thing," Horace grunted. "That leg's busted an ya ain't movin'."

"Well, Brett," Mr. Tyler reported. "Looks as if you'll be fine. You two are pretty lucky. A good cut on your head and some cracked ribs. We'll be shippin' ya off ta Doc Blevin's for repairs and then home for healin' time."

"Pa, do I have to go back home?"

"No, Son. We'll go back to the Tylers'."

Brett and his father were placed in the wagon and taken back to the camp. The ride was painfully rough.

"Does it hurt much, Pa?" he asked.

"Quite a bit at first. But I'm getting used to it." His voice was tight with pain.

Back at camp, the wagon was parked in the shade under the end of the mess tent.

"Can we get out?" Brett wondered.

"You're likely to get dizzy," Mr. Tyler said. "Ya best lie still 'til we can fix up a bunk in the caboose."

An hour dragged by after the wagon had brought the boy and his father back from the accident. The crews had gone back to the slopes to finish the day's cutting. The pulpwood loads had been taken down, along with a report of the accident and the need for the doctor. Only two of the log loads were completed by the end of the afternoon. The third had a partial load and the remaining cars were empty.

Horace had stayed close the whole time, offering water or coffee as the two became thirsty. Bill Tyler was in and out, checking on Brett and his father, chatting a while, then going back to supervise work. Horace explained their injuries. Brett's father had a bad break in the lower right leg. Brett had a couple of cracked ribs and a cut on his head.

The shrill call of the "Scott's" whistle announced it had nearly arrived to take down the last load. It also signaled the end of the working day.

This being Friday, most of the crew would be going down on the train and were busy stowing tools and gathering clean clothes and travel packs.

In the wagon Mr. Tompkins spoke to Brett. "Jay's crew should be on. He'll probably have old Doc, too."

"Pa? It hurts worse. I'm cold," he shivered, but determined to bear the pain without crying.

The sound of the brakes and of escaping air and steam was distinct as the train stopped. A commotion of voices moved toward the tent. Mr. Tompkins sat up as they approached.

"Teddy." It was Doc Blevins. "Bob Leary told me about the accident when he came down." Even as he spoke he was checking over Brett's injuries. "As soon as Jay has switched over the train, we'll get you two on board."

"Horace," Doc instructed, "get some blankets." The June sun was baking the area in the eighties, but Brett's body had suddenly become cold and clammy from shock and loss of blood. Doc used one blanket to make a pad for Brett's head and wrapped him up in a second one. Meanwhile the train was being remade for the return trip. The "Scott" had brought one additional car, the company mixed coach. All ten flats would be taken back since the partial and empties would cause scheduling problems if left for next week. Jay and Scot left the train and went to check on Mr. Tompkins and his son. Most of the camp had already gathered around the wagon for a progress report.

Doc saw the two men coming from the engine. "The train's ready, men. Sean, will you ask Dan Seegers to have the baggage door open on the caboose. Everyone who's goin' in with us go on and board. Bill Tyler will help us get these two on."

The men left who were riding down. Those who were tending the camp for the weekend moved away to take care of the horses or finish cleaning up for dinner.

"Doc, how're they doin'?" questioned Scot.

Blevins stepped aside. "Bill, take the wagon over. We'll be right along," he instructed. Then turning to the two, "Brett's not too good jest now. He's gone shocky from loss of blood. His pa's not great, mind ya, but okay. Bad break in his leg. They should both mend. Come on." Doc started toward the train. "Let's head down."

The trip down was long. Jay kept the train running smoothly, slow enough to avoid rocking on the uneven rail joints. Mr. Tompkins and his son had been placed in the crew bunks in the caboose. All the doors and windows had been opened for maximum ventilation. Brett had become unconscious. His father wanted to sit up and keep an eye on him, but Doc had insisted he stay down for his own well-being and had braced the splinted leg with blankets so it would not be jarred.

Adam and his mother were waiting at the station with a wagon when the train arrived. Sean and Lyle helped Mr. Tyler and Doc transport the patients over to the house where they would be treated and looked after.

At the station, Bob Leary's crew had returned from the afternoon freight run and, hearing of the delay, had gone ahead and made up the Friday evening train. Jay spotted the log cars on the mill siding and picked up the empties. He returned to the station where Bob took over to put the equipment away. Jay's crew then moved over to the evening coach to prepare for departure to Arlee. The train would lay over in Arlee and return in the morning. Number Twenty-One finally departed around seven in the evening, about an hour late of schedule.

At the Tyler house Brett's injuries had been bathed, his head stitched, dressings put on, and his ribs rewrapped. His clothes had been exchanged for his nightshirt, and he was put to bed. The boy remained unconscious through it all. While Doc set Mr. Tompkins' leg, Mrs. Tyler stayed with Brett. Adam helped out by carrying things back and forth from the kitchen and by spelling his mother while she fixed dinner.

Doc Blevins stayed the night. But by ten in the evening it was evident that Brett was resting easier. His skin was warmer and he was sleeping comfortably.

Jason's Trip from Arlee

The mist dotted the window pane spreading slowly downward as its density grew. Light rain and fog gave the world outside an eerie aspect. A small ghostly hunchbacked figure glided through the fog. As it came closer and clearer it was easily recognizable as Jason carrying an armload of wood. He burst noisily into the bright warm kitchen. The kitchen air sizzled with the warm aroma of bacon. Mrs. Johnston was busy getting breakfast ready for the hotel guests, many of whom would have to be at the station by 7:45 for the morning trains.

"Ma." Jason dropped the wood in the wood box. "It's nearly time for Jay ta come in. I'm goin' over ta see what news he brings of Brett."

"See ya later, son. Let us know how he's doin'" she said.

Five days had passed since Jay had brought news of the accident on the mountain. Jason had sent a letter back telling his friend to get well and how he was sorry to hear of the accident. Each day since then, he had met the train to check with Jay on Brett's progress. Both Brett and his father were up and around, but confined to the house to take it easy. Mr. Tompkins would be back to the office by mid-week, restricted to his desk mostly. But after two weeks of mending, he would be permitted on the mountain if he took it easy. Brett's stitches would be out by week's end and he would be able to go anywhere as long as he took it easy and didn't do any lifting for a couple of weeks.

Jason grabbed a piece of bacon and folded it into a biscuit as he headed toward the front hall. He walked across the street to the station platform, and across the platform to a post near the track. Here he was under the roof out of the rain, and away from the crowd enough to be able to see down the track as he waited. The train from Summit had backed up the main north of the station area, its ghostly figure like a shadow in the fog, its lamp like an evil eye gleaming on the track in front of the platform.

Number Twenty-One's whistle cut through the mist. The pounding of its pistons drew closer as its bell began to ring. The rhythmic pounding slowed as the sound crept up alongside the parked train. Jason saw the rays of the head-lamp ripple through the mist followed by the shape of the locomotive. Even as the train slowed on the passing track, Jason ran toward the engine. Dan waved a greeting which the boy acknowledged as he reached the engine cab. The train stopped, Dan stepped down and opened the coupling separating the engine from the train, and Jason scrambled up the steps to the cab. Number Twenty-One eased back onto the main and headed toward the yard to be turned.

"Mornin', Jason," Jay greeted. Before the boy could ask he reported, "Brett's doin' fine. I stopped again last evenin'. He says 'hi' and sends you this note. His pa goes back ta work today. He and I talked last night and he, too, sends a note. It's inside."

He handed the boy the envelope. Jason scrambled up onto Scot's box to open the note and read what it said. He studied the lines carefully and his eyes were wide with excitement as he finished.

"Yippee!" he shouted. "Wow! I can't believe it!"

"What's all the excitement?" Scot asked.

"Brett's pa has invited me ta spend a week with 'em! Oh, Scot, Jay, it's so great!" There were tears of joy in his eyes.

"That's right," Jay confirmed. He brushed a sooty sleeve across each eye. "We talked it over last night. I've another letter from Mr. Tompkins for yer folks."

The engine slowed as it approached the yard switch. A man standing by the switch waved the engine through. The wheels rumbled across the junction to the yard track and proceeded through two more switches leading to the turntable. Jay centered Number Twenty-One on the table and set the brakes. He leaned out the window and waved to the yard men at either end of the table. They leaned into the poles and the track began to rotate as the locomotive was turned around. The track was lined up again and the yard crew waved all clear. Jay acknowledged with two short blasts on the whistle. He eased the engine forward, off the table and proceeded toward the water tower. Scot and Jason climbed up to the water fill on the tender tank, opened the lid, and pulled the spout down. Water gushed into the fill hole, splashing around the opening and dousing both their pant legs and shoes. When the tank was full, they released the spout, which sprang back up into the air, capped the opening, and returned to the cab.

Jay spoke as he cleared the yard switch and headed back to the station. "As soon as the train is spotted on the siding, we'll check with John Abrams and let him know we'll be late leavin'. Scot will move into the station when it's time. You and me'll go over to see your folks and get ya packed."

The Summit train had backed up north of the switch so that Twenty-One could back in to hook up at the other end of the train. Dan was waiting. The train was coupled and backed onto the siding as the Summit train pulled onto the pass track to await the Pine Bluff and Truckee trains at eight o'clock. Jay and Jason climbed down and walked across the station platform to the stationmaster's office. After checking in with Mr. Abrams, they continued on to the hotel.

"Mornin', Nancy. Mornin', Hank," Jay greeted as the two entered the kitchen. Mr. Johnston was just reaching for his hat to leave. "Hank, you got a minute? I've a letter here for you both from Teddy Tompkins."

"How is he?" Mrs. Johnston asked, "and how's his son doin'?"

"They're both comin' along fine." He handed the letter to Mr. Johnston.

"They've asked me to come visit for a week!" Jason burst in, face beaming with happiness.

Mr. Johnston looked up from the letter. "That's right, Nancy. Teddy writes that Jason can stay with them and that his train fare has already been taken care of."

"Can I go?" Jason asked.

"I'm not sure," his father winked at his mother, "that your ma can handle things here without your help."

"We'd manage," Mrs. Johnston cut in quickly as tears started up in her son's eyes. "Run up and find the old suitcase. I'll help you pack. Hank, get Jay a cup o' coffee while we're gone."

Jason disappeared up the back steps. His mother followed. The men turned to the table to talk of the trip, to share news, and to enjoy their coffee.

*   *   *

The fog had lifted some and a steady drizzle fell as Jay slowed for the turn before Chamber's Crossing. Jason was surprised to see Jamie climb aboard. The older boy was dripping wet from the rain. He hung his slicker on a hook in the back of the cab and crouched in front of the firebox to dry off some. The boys were introduced. Jamie reported the trestle in good shape, but some rotting ties would need tending before long.

"Here, Scot, let me rake her down," Jamie offered. "It might help me dry faster."

The fireman handed over the long iron fire rake. Jamie opened the firebox door and reached in to level out the ashes and hot coals. Then he threw on another half dozen shovels of coal. Scot checked the gauges. The train was making good time and had picked up about fifteen minutes with the help of short stops at Blakesville and Kingston. Jay had explained their lateness to Jamie. He had wondered what happened, but figured the weather was the problem.

"Almost there," Jay announced as Jamie put his slicker back on and moved to the steps to throw the switch. Jason watched the move with interest as the train crossed onto the passing track for Snow Shoe.

"Jamie, you take the bell goin' in," Scot said as Jay sounded the whistle to announce their arrival. Jamie set the bell to ringing. The train eased to a stop at the platform.

Jason quickly descended the steps. "Thanks, Jay. See ya later." He hurried to grab his bag from the baggage door.

"Hi, Jason!" Brett was coming from the station door.

"Brett! Gee I'm glad to see ya again." He ran to meet him. He wanted to hug his friend like a long lost brother, but caught himself for fear of hurting Brett's ribs.

"Hey, Little Brother. You two wanta drown like rats? Get up here where it's dry some." It was Adam calling from the Herald's delivery wagon. "Mr. Clanton said I could borrow this and deliver ya home. He doesn't mean for me ta let you two ta be sponges."

Brett and Jason ran to the wagon and climbed up beside Adam. He slapped the reins gently and started up Main Street.

"This is Adam Tyler," Brett introduced. "Me an' my pa live with his folks. Since I got hurt he's taken to callin' me Little Brother. But he watches after me more like a mother."

"Nice ta meet ya, Jason," Adam said. "Really, I hafta look after this friend o' yours so's he minds what Doc says. Once I dump ya at the house, though, he's yours. I gotta go back to the Herald and help Evan set type."

"I'll look ta him like a hawk," Jason laughed.

"That's all I need," Brett chuckled. "Another mother. This time a hawk."

All three laughed at this. The wagon turned the corner and pulled into the lane at the Tyler place. Brett and Jason hopped down and ran for the porch. Adam turned the wagon and started out.

"See ya at dinner," he waved. The splashing of hoofs and wheels faded down the street.

"Come on," Brett said. He led the way through the house to the kitchen. Jason was introduced to Mrs. Tyler who promptly served them both some hot soup and biscuits.

Afterwards she instructed, "Brett, you get yerself inta some dry clothes and show Jason to the spare room."

"Please, ma'am, might Jason share my room?"

"All right. When Adam gets home we'll see about gettin' out his father's old army cot if Jason wants to use it."

"I'd like that fine," Jason assured.

The younger boy's bag was unpacked and his clothes were stowed in the drawers with Brett's. The two of them shared the news of what each had done during the past weeks. Jason examined the scar on Brett's head from which the stitches had been remover the previous afternoon. The rain continued for the rest of the day and confined them to the house. They amused themselves with game after game of checkers until Adam came in.

The front door opened and the sound of squishing feet passed down the hall toward the kitchen. Brett and Jason looked up from their game at the kitchen table.

"Boy, talk about drowning," Brett burst out laughing.

"That bad, huh," Adam smiled.

"I'll say," Jason added. "You must be a mother duck."

"Maybe it's not as bad as it's quacked up to be," Adam challenged laughingly as he hung his coat by the stove. They all laughed.

"Adam," his mother broke in. "You best hang the rest of your clothes there, too, and get inta somethin' dry."

He took off his shirt and threw it at Brett. "Catch quick, Little Brother." The impact sent water splashing as Brett reached out to catch and squinted his eyes to keep out the drops. Jason was next as the dripping wet pants went flying his way.

"See you guys shortly." Adam retreated in his johns, heading toward his room for dry clothes.

Jason and Brett looked at each other with water dripping from face and hands. "Let's get him," Jason suggested.

"Yeh," Brett agreed. They dropped the wet clothes and charged for the stairs.

"Brett! Jason!" Mrs. Tyler called. But they were gone. She smiled to herself as she picked up the wet clothes and hung them on the pegs by the stove.

Charging footsteps clattered up the stairs to Adam's room. He had barely pulled on a dry pair of johns when they jumped him and wrestled him to the floor. Brett screamed with pain and the commotion ceased instantly. He lay on the floor whimpering as Adam and Jason rolled aside and knelt beside him. Mrs. Tyler raced up the stairs.

"Adam!" she called. "What happened?"

"Brett's hurt." He put his hand on Brett's shoulder as the younger boy pushed himself over onto his back.

"You okay?" he asked as his mother burst into the room.

Brett nodded his head yes as tears rolled down his face and he winced with pain. He forced a smile. "Guess I forgot, Big Brother. Give me a minute ta catch my breath."

"I'm sorry," Jason sniffed. "It's all my fault. It was my idea." Mrs. Tyler reached down to pull him to his feet.

"Now, Jason, don't fret none. Brett'll be fine. We all hafta keep a mind ta being careful." She knelt down and gave him a hug. "I'll take the rest of Adam's wet clothes. Maybe he'll show ya his collection."

Mrs. Tyler left as Brett caught his breath and crawled to the bed. He sat there on the floor with his back against it waiting for Adam to finish dressing. Jason sat down beside him. In true showmanship fashion, Adam went through his collection for both of them.

"And here, my friends, is a rail spike, taken with my own hands from beside the track near South Camp."

*   *   *

Doc Blevins stopped after dinner to check on Mr. Tompkins' progress his first day back. He checked Brett's ribs after hearing of the rough treatment he'd given them and admonished him for his carelessness. He added that fortunately there had been no damage.

At bedtime Brett and Jason looked out toward the mountain. But it was hard to see in the continuing rain, so they climbed into Brett's bed to talk.

"So much has happened," observed Jason, "that it doesn't seem like the same day."

"I know," Brett agreed. "My first day here was like that."

Adam ducked in to say good night. He bounced lightly onto the bed and sat near their feet. "You guys sleep good," he said. "Maybe if it stops rainin', we can go fishin' tomorrow. I know a good spot on Lawrence Creek."

"Sounds great," the other two agreed. Adam hopped back down to the floor.

"Best git ta bed." He started to the door. "Night."

"Night, Adam," each called after him.

"He's right," Brett said. Jason climbed into his cot. "How is it?" Brett asked.

"Different," came the reply. "Tell you come mornin'."

Brett blew out the lamp and crawled back into bed. They talked on briefly. But soon each mumbled a good night to the other as they drifted off to sleep.

GONE FISHING

A light mist hung on the air. High grey clouds moved swiftly across the sky from the northeast. Adam led the way as the three barefoot boys hiked up the muddy lane behind the barn. Periodically they would stop to turn over stones or rotting logs to hunt for worms which they would scoop up and add to the collection in the old tin can which Brett was carrying. Each boy carried a pole equipped with a length of feed bag string, a light weight, a cork float, and a small hook. Adam had a pack of extra hooks in his pocket.

"This looks like a good place," Jason announced. His toes sank in the squishy mud as he squatted down and rolled aside a perspective stone. Three worms scurried toward holes. Jason grabbed a large night crawler and held it up triumphantly. "Here's a fat one," he called.

Brett held out the can and his friend deposited his trophy. Jason wiped his muddy hands on his shirttail as they moved on. The lane opened into a hillside pasture. Weeds and brush had overrun the grass and glistened wet in the mist. Cutting across toward the eastern edge of the meadow, the boys' pants were quickly soaked with moisture. The three boys climbed across the rails at the fence line and followed Adam along a winding trail through dense underbrush. The trail wound around trees on an upgrade for several hundred yards. Ducking through the underbrush, the group came out on the creek bank.

"There's a pretty good hole around that bend up there," Adam pointed. They slopped along the trail until they arrived at the place Adam had selected. Laying their gear against a fallen tree branch, they knelt in the grass by the edge of the water and peered into the rain fed current for signs of fish. Some minnows were spotted around the rocks. Then some larger fish were seen lounging lazily in a back eddy.

"Shall we try here?" Brett asked.

"Looks good," Adam agreed.

Brett dumped some worms on the ground. Each selected one and pushed it onto his hook. Brett put the rest back into the can. The lines were dropped in and each boy made himself comfortable as he sat in the wet grass and waited for a bite. Jason's float went under.

"Got one!" he announced as he jerked on his line. It came up empty. "Darn," he whispered. "Pulled too soon."

They waited awhile longer. Adam's line went under. He tugged lightly, then pulled gently, drawing his line toward the water's edge.

"It's on," Brett said.

Adam lifted his line to the grass and landed a flopping fish. He quickly pinned it to the ground with one hand and eased the hook from its mouth with the other.

"A bit small," he commented. "Maybe six inches."

Brett and Jason's lines came alive at the same time and each landed a lively catch. Jason's fish was the largest, at about eight inches. All three were placed in a feed sack which had been brought along for that purpose. They put their lines back in and waited. Four more small fish were caught before a large trout snapped at Jason's line and pulled it under a rock as he tugged on the pole. It stuck tight.

"Darn, it's snagged," he complained.

"Let me try it, Jason," Brett offered. He worked the line to either side, but it refused to give.

"I'll get it," Adam stated. "Hold my line, Little Brother." He handed the pole to Brett.

Adam rolled his pant legs up above his knees, then slipped into the water. Inching his way toward the rock he gradually moved to deeper water. The current swirled just below the boy's pants at first. But by the time he reached the rock, it was nearly to his waist.

"The rain's made the water deeper 'n I thought," the older boy said.

He had to kneel under water to reach the hook. It was freed. Adam stood up shaking water from his hair.

"Jason!" Adam spit water. "Next time you get your own hook!" He splashed back toward the bank, crawled out, and flopped down in the grass. Jason pulled his line out of the water.

"I'm sorry, Adam." He choked back a sob. "I'd a done it if you'd said."

"It's okay," Adam comforted. "It's no use fishin' here any more. We might as well go swimmin' instead." He got up and took his pole from Brett.

They moved all their fishing gear back to the tree branch. Adam draped his dripping shirt over a limb that stuck up. Brett and Jason hung theirs up also.

"Don't dive," Adam warned. "Too many rocks."

The boys jumped in and splashed around. Adam leaned back against the current and tried to swim upstream against its swiftness. Brett found that any stroke caused pain, so he settled himself to wading. He worked his way upstream to a narrows where the water rushed between the rocks, and sat against the tumbling torrent.

"Hey, this feels neat," he called.

Jason tried it out and agreed. He leaned back and let the current push him downstream. Adam, too, tried it out. Then he and Jason took turns letting the rushing waters cast them from the rocks. After a half hour of this play, the three of them crawled out onto the bank. Their wet hair was plastered against their faces. They ran their hands back pushing their hair up into frozen waves and wringing water down their necks and behind their ears.

A rustling noise up stream caught their attention. As they watched quietly, a buck and a doe wandered into the water. The doe drank as the buck surveyed the surroundings for danger, The boys kept real still. The buck drank, then the two crossed the water and disappeared into the woodland.

"Wow!" Jason whispered softly.

A stiff breeze arose and they shivered in the dampness. Adam glanced up toward the sky.

"It's getting darker and the wind has picked up," he observed. Large drops of rain began to fall. Thunder rumbled in the distance. "Sounds like a storm's comin' on. Let's head for home."

They pulled on their shirts, picked up the fishing paraphernalia, and turned downstream toward home. Adam led the way back across the trail to the meadow and the lane. The rain began to pelt them with some force and quickly turned the lane into a slippery mud slick. It was downhill all the way which made going easier, except when Jason slipped and sat down with a sudden muddy splash. When the trio arrived at the house, Mrs. Tyler intercepted them at the back door.

"Not a step further!" she called from the porch steps. The three drenched and mud-splashed boys stopped at the foot of the steps. "Put your gear on the porch. You can tend it later. Then put those muddy clothes on the line and wash off at the well. How could you be such a mess!"

The boys laid their gear on the porch along with the sack of fish and began to slip out of their shirts and pants.

"When you've washed off, get in by the kitchen stove to dry and get warmed up." A bolt of lightning lashed out at the mountain as the air crashed with thunder. "And hurry it along." Mrs. Tyler went into the house to find towels for each.

Adam, Brett, and Jason flung their clothes over the line and dashed toward the well. Adam drew up a bucket of water. He threw part at Jason's legs.

"Rub the mud off and turn around," Adam instructed. Jason only managed to streak the mud down the length of his body. "Here, wash your hands first."

Jason washed them in the bucket then pulled up the legs of his longjohns. A second dousing was successful. Adam threw more water on the back of Jason's legs with enough force to help loosen the mud so that it would rub off more easily. Brett took his turn, then Jason drew water for Adam. The storm was growing in intensity as the trio dashed dripping into the kitchen. The fish were forgotten.

They took the towels Mrs. Tyler handed them and began rubbing the water from their skin. The boys huddled close to the warmth of the stove. Water ran down their legs and dripped from their hair, puddling around their feet where they stood. Adam's mother got another towel and began drying Brett's head with a vigorous rubbing.

"Ow!" he complained. She pulled back quickly to be gentle around the scarring from the area of the stitches.

"Hold still. You'll be lucky ya don't catch yer death of cold." She proceeded to each in turn. Adam's mother left the room briefly to return with three quilts. As each boy finished drying, she handed him a quilt.

"Here, wrap yerselves in these and sit by the stove while I get on some soup." After handing each of the boys a quilt to wrap up in, she placed a chair for each by the stove. Each in turn slipped out of his johns and wrapped up in his quilt to sit in his chair and get warm.

The wind picked up and began to whistle in the chimney and to rattle the windows. Lightning flashed outside followed by long rumblings and crashing of thunder.

"That ol' storm sure come up fast," Jason commented as he pulled the quilt around him.

"Good thing we were comin' in anyway," Brett added. "I'd sure hate ta be up on the mountain in all that lightning."

Mrs. Tyler handed each a mug of soup. "Drink it slowly. It's hot." She checked the forehead of each. "Ya seem healthy enough. But jest ta be safe, I want each of ya ta stay put till you're warm clean through. Then ya put on dry clothes and stay here in the kitchen where it's warmest."

"Ma," Adam asked. "Can we fix our fish for lunch?"

"Yes, son. But I'll fetch 'em in and leave 'em on the drain board for ya. You stay put and get dry. Then get on dry clothes before ya go fixin yer fish."

* * *

The fish smelled good as they fried in the pan. Following fish and biscuit lunch, Adam got out the checkers game and they took turns playing during the first of the afternoon. Later they retreated to Adam's room to watch the storm from his window and to watch for the arrival of Brett and Adam's fathers.

When the men came in, Mr. Tompkins had letters for Brett and Jason. The two sat at the kitchen table and read their letters quietly to themselves while Adam sat by and watched. He suddenly felt very much left out. He didn't have anyone to get mail from.

"Any news?" Adam asked.

"Ma says she misses us," Brett offered. "She also says ... never mind, read it to ya."

Brett read his letter for both of them. Jason did the same. Brett's mother was closing up the house and leaving to visit her mother. She had received Brett's letter and was glad he was having a good time, though she couldn't wait to see him and his father back home again. The Johnstons wrote that they were keeping busy, they were fine, and they missed Jason and hoped he was having a good time. They also sent a hello to Brett and his dad and a thank you to the Tylers for having Jason.

"Dinner's nearly ready," Mrs. Tyler announced.

Conversation was lively during dinner as the boys shared their fishing adventure along with the deer sighting, and the men told of storm damage on the mountain. A falling tree nearly landed on a bunk car. Another did land across the tracks causing a delay while the track was cleared. One section of roadbed had washed so badly, the tracks had slipped. If Jay hadn't been going so slowly, the train would probably have wrecked.

After dinner was cleared away and the dishes finished, the adults retired to the living room and the boys to the kitchen. Brett and Jason worked on writing letters home. Adam cleaned up the fishing poles and wrapped the lines. Jason wrote that he was having a good time. Brett wrote of the accident, of his friend's visit, of fishing, and of his wish that his mother would come.

It had been a tiring day. The continuing storm brought early darkness. The boys were ready to retire early. Jason and Brett gave their letters to Brett's father to be mailed. The tired trio turned in for the night.

DAY OF THE STORM

As Friday dawned, the storm continued to rage. Work on the mountain was suspended for the day, resulting in the closing of the sawmill as well. The morning train to South Camp would consist of the mixed coach, caboose, and a flatcar loaded with rails, ties, and track tools. The train would also carry logging tools and rope for clearing fallen debris from the track. Some of the men from the sawmill hired on for the day to help as needed with track repair and clearing work. Only one trip would be made this day to clear the right of way and to pick up anyone coming off the mountain for the weekend. The men at South Camp would be permitted to leave early due to the storm. Adam was off to work at the Herald. Brett and Jason would spend the morning with Mr. Tyler on the train. Mr. Tompkins would remain at the office.

Rain fell 1n sheets as the two boys and Mr. Tyler dashed from the office to the waiting train. They scrambled up the steps and into the protective dryness of the caboose. The supplies for next week had been stacked in the freight room and glistened wet with rain water. Puddles of runoff marked the floor around the boxes. The lamp was lit in the crew area and the stove had been lit to help dry out the dampness in the air. A pot of coffee simmered on the stove top. Crew men David Jackson and Buddy Wetherby rode the back platform to work the switches. Mr. Tyler and the boys sat at the table. The boys watched out the window while Mr. Tyler sipped a cup of coffee and went over the list of added help for the trip. Jamie Rhodes was on with two of the regular maintenance crew plus a half dozen extras from the mill. They had all settled in the coach. The "Scott's" whistle sounded twice and the train began to move. After the switch was cleared, the boys saw Mr. Jackson run ahead and climb into the engine cab.

"Mr. Tyler," Brett said. "We're going out back to ride with Mr. Wetherby."

"Okay, boys. Be careful."

The boys walked back through the freight room and out onto the platform.

"Hi, boys," Mr. Wetherby greeted. "Be sure to hang on tight. It's likely we'll hit some pretty rough track."

"Do ya think the bad spot comin' down yesterday will have washed out?" Brett asked.

"Hard tellin'," came the reply. "We'll find out soon's we get there."

The train continued up the creek valley. The water broiled in Stewart Creek as the rain-fed current rushed downhill. The water had risen several feet and was brown with dirt carved from along its banks. The slow, steady working of the "Scott's" pistons echoed across the creek bed. Black smoke and the smell of burning wood hung heavy on the air. Cinders mixed with the falling rain, leaving black smudges on skin or clothes. Brett watched the rail pass through the space between the platform on which he stood and the flatcar following behind. The rain, the mist, the smoke, the rumbling wheels and chugging pistons, the smell of wood smoke and dampness, all combined to give the mountain a character of mystery.

Three sharp blasts of the whistle struck the air and echoed in the mist and rain. Just as suddenly, the train slowed sharply, then came to a halt. The three scurried down the steps and looked up the track. Mr. Tyler stepped down from the front steps as Jamie and the work crew poured out of the front car. The cause of the delay was a large tree across the tracks.

"You two get back aboard and stay dry," the trainman instructed. "we'll be clear shortly."

He went ahead with Mr. Tyler to help the rest of the crew clear the track. Mr. Tyler disappeared into the coach. Seconds later the baggage door rolled open and he was visible passing tools down to the workmen. As the engine waited restlessly with steam hissing and rumbling in its belly, and black smoke rising in a column only to be held down by the heavy wet air, the ring of axes and saws began to call out. The fallen giant was quickly dismembered until all that remained were stripped twigs and leaves and a scattering of sawdust and wood chips. A sudden silence filled the air as the tools were put away and the sweat and rain-soaked men climbed back on board. Jamie supervised in the baggage area and left the door open for the next stop which was inevitable. Mr. Tyler and Mr. Wetherby returned to the caboose. Two short whistle blasts shattered the brief silence and the train eased into forward motion.

The train proceeded on its course to the switchback. After about ten minutes of travel, the air above the left side of the caboose exploded with the sound of crashing wood and splintering branches. Jason dashed to the steps to see what was happening. Brett ducked into the doorway for fear of being struck down. A large section of tree smashed to the ground not twenty feet from the train.

"Wow! That was close!" Jason exclaimed. The car jerked suddenly over rough track. Jason lost his balance and fell on the steps. A quick grab by Mr. Wetherby saved the boy from falling off the steps to the moving ground below. Jason felt a sudden emptiness inside as if someone had unexpectedly pulled a plug causing his insides to drain away. The man helped a badly shaken boy back to his feet.

"Ya better go in and sit down. You're turnin' white."

"Come on," Brett said in a very subdued tone. "Let's go in."

The two went in and found a seat at the table. Mr. Tyler had been watching track from the front platform and came in when he saw the boys.

"What's wrong, Jason? You look powerful sick," he observed.

"He lost his footin' and nearly fell off, sir," Brett explained.

"How do you feel, Jason?" Mr. Tyler asked.

The boy looked up at the man. There were beads of sweat on his face. "I don't feel good at all," he replied. The train continued to rock down the track.

"You best lie down a bit until ya get your color back." He helped him into a bunk.

"I think I'll lie down, too," Brett said. He climbed in with Jason putting his head on a blanket at the foot of the bed. The rocking motion continued and the boy had to brace himself to avoid pain in his chest.

The train finally slowed for the switchback. It paused a couple of minutes while Mr. Wetherby threw the switch. Easing into reverse it continued its travel up the mountain toward South Camp.

During the first mile from the switch, the track was considerably smoother. Jason and Brett felt better as their stomachs recovered from the earlier rough motion and Jason's nervousness left him from the close call and fright of nearly falling off the open platform. The boys were up and sitting at the table. Raindrops streaked the window pane as they splashed against the outside of the glass and left sooty streaks. The rumble of the wheels could be felt through the floor boards as the train rolled at a slow, steady speed. The crew kept a careful watch on the track for weakness or washout. The whistle sounded three short blasts and the train slowed as Mr. Wetherby burst in through the rear door and hollered toward the boys from the freight room.

"You got your answer on the washout, Brett. Come see fer yerself."

The boys scrambled to the back door. Brakes squealed and the train stopped. Stepping out onto the platform the boys saw a mud slick and scattered ties and rails where the roadbed once had been. The flatcar rested on the last pair of rails still in place. Some thirty yards ahead the rails resumed their normal course.

"Gee!" Jason exclaimed. "How're we goin' to cross that?"

Men from the coach began to gather around the flatcar. "You two jest watch," the trainman answered as he climbed across to the flat. "We'll have that track relaid. It may take a while, though."

"Jamie." Mr. Tyler had climbed aboard the flat and began to pass down tools and instructions. "Take the mill crew with shovels and throw down earth from uphill of the wash."

Jamie and the mill crew moved to the hillside and began to shovel the earth into the roadbed to build it back up.

"Jerry, Jake, Bud, and Dave, salvage what ya can of the ties and get them placed." Mr. Tyler handed tools to Bud Wetherby who jumped down to join the other three on the slope.

The running water and slippery mud made progress awkwardly slow. The ties were dragged into place and rocked down into the soft earth.

It took over a half hour to span the washout. But finally the link was made. It took ten of the men, working in pairs, to pull each rail from the car and set it in place. As each rail was lined up, the connectors were bolted on and the rail spiked down. Then its mate was gauged, connected, and spiked down. Gradually the gap was shortened until at last, the final link was closed. The tools were stowed back in the bin on the flat and the crew climbed back aboard the train. Each man was dripping wet from sweat and rain, with shoes and trousers caked in mud. Mr. Wetherby and Mr. Tyler joined the boys on the platform. The foreman signaled to the engine. Two short whistle blasts acknowledged and the wheels began to turn again.

Cautiously the train continued its trek toward South Camp. After less than a quarter mile, it stopped again so that a tree could be cleared from the track. The trip was resumed. About a half mile north of the camp the train was rounding a bend when the flatcar suddenly slipped sideways with a banging of iron and a splintering of wood.

Mr. Leary saw the slip from the engine cab and locked the brakes instantly. The train jolted to a dead stop. The boys were thrown against the railings as Mr. Wetherby lost his footing and fell to the platform. Brett winced with pain, gripping the handrail tightly. Jason saw his friend's knuckles turn white and looked to see what was wrong.

"You okay, Brett?" he asked.

"Yeh," came a breathless reply. "Caught me by surprise."

Mr. Tyler came out the door as the trainman got back on his feet. "What happened?"

"Seems the rail's slipped," Mr. Wetherby replied.

They climbed down to take a look. Everybody came running to see what had happened. Indeed, the downhill rails had ripped loose of the ties and slipped sideways. The connector joints had held and the wheels from the flat had fallen to the wooden ties and broken some of them.

"What da ya think, Bob?" Mr. Tyler asked. "Can ya pull her back on and we'll spike it back down?"

"It's worth a try," the engineer replied. "Sure looks like a possibility."

"You men stand by," Mr. Tyler instructed. "If we clear, we'll nail the rail back down and be on our way. Okay, Bob, let's have a go at it."

The engine crew returned to the cab. The group watched expectantly as the engineer eased in the throttle and the train began to drift forward. Jamie stepped closer to check the wheels to be sure they were riding back up onto the rail. The wheels came in contact with the rails and began to lift off the ties as the rail squeezed in on them. They approached a connector. BANG! The bolts snapped and the rail sprung sideways.

"Watch out!" Jamie called as he jumped backwards from the track. He lost his footing and fell on the roadbed. "Ahhh!" the boy screamed painfully. The rail landed with a sickening crunch on his foot.

"Get it off!" Mr. Tyler yelled. Ten pairs of hands grabbed at and lifted the end of the rail as he dragged Jamie out from under it. Brett ran toward the engine to tell Mr. Leary to stop. But it wasn't necessary. He'd been watching all along and had stopped as soon as the rail had given way.

"It hurts somethin' fierce, Mr. Tyler!" Jamie cried.

"I'm sure it does, Son. It's pretty badly busted up. We'll get ya into one of the bunks. Horace'll wrap it when we get in." He turned to see who was near. "Jason, you and Brett fix up that bunk you used. Spread a blanket and get a spare for padding." The boys hurried to comply. "Bud, Dave, help me get him on board. Be carefull with that foot."

Jamie was light to move. He cried out when they moved his foot. There was no way to prevent the pain or to ease it. Inside the caboose he was made as comfortable as possible. Jason and Brett sat with him while the crew worked to get the train back on the track.

Using a ramp constructed from ties, the wheels were lifted and guided back onto the rails. The broken connector was replaced and the rails spiked back down. The train completed its trip to the camp without further incident.

The stopover at South Camp was brief. The materials and supplies were quickly unloaded from the caboose and stowed in their proper places in the kitchen or supply tents. Horace wrapped Jamie's foot.

Jason and Brett watched from their seats at the table. Mr. Tyler stood by as did Mr. Wetherby. Horace's hands moved gently and carefully.

"Bad break," he muttered. "Yer gonna be down several weeks."

There was quiet while he worked except for the pattering of rain on the roof, the splashing of the runoff, and the crackle of the stove fire.

"Done," Horace stated. Patting the boy on the shoulder as he stood up, he added in a rare hint of affection, "Take care." He turned to leave and caught sight of the boys.

"Vou mendin', boy?" he asked Brett.

"Yes, sir. Thank you." Brett was pleased to be noticed.

"Jest bein' sure I'll be getting' my help back," the cook grunted.

He limped out and was gone.

"Time ta get goin'," Mr. Tyler observed. "I'll be seein' ta departure. You boys stay put. Bud, stay here in case you're needed." The foreman left.

"Brett," Jamie spoke. "Ya musta hurt pretty bad when you were hit by that tree."

"It seems a long time back," Brett said. "But it sure did hurt. I've never hurt like that before."

"Me neither. Does it still hurt?"

"Sometimes. When we stopped and I hit the rail, it hurt."

Five minutes had passed since Mr. Tyler had left, when the "Scott's" whistle signaled they were moving out. The train eased forward and began the slow trip back to Snow Shoe. The repairs held for the return trip. The only stop was made when the train paused at the switch. From there it descended to the station where men leaving for the weekend disembarked along with the mill crew who had helped on the trip up. Mr. Tyler went for Doc Blevins who brought his buggy to move Jamie. After Jamie had been safely delivered home, the foreman returned to the train. The boys, the track crew men, and Mr. Tyler returned with the train crew to the company yards.

GETTING OUT THE HERALD

The young man pulled on the press lever, sandwiching the paper between the flats of type. It squeaked under the strain and snapped back when the pressure was released. The bed was rolled out and opened as experienced hands lifted the sheet and read it over.

"Yer doin' fine, Earl," Mr. Clanton complimented. "Here, Adam. You can hang this one. Let's run it."

Earl Lambert was a young man in his twenties. While he wasn't really fat, his face seemed a bit pudgy in the cheeks. He had sideburns down to his jawline and a circle of thinning dark hair on top. The apron he wore was smudged with printer's ink. His hands were kept wiped on a rag to prevent dirtying of the paper.

The three of them began the work cycle as the last June issue came off the press. Adam laid the blank paper in the bed. Mr. Clanton closed it and ran it up under the press. Earl pressed the imprint. Mr. Clanton rolled the bed back and opened it. Adam pulled the printed sheet and laid on a clean one. The cycle repeated as Adam hung the new paper to dry. The first part of the morning had been spent printing the advertiser sheet that went into the center of the Herald. The news section was printed last so any last minute news could be added if important enough, such as the piece about the storm damage and derailment that Mr. Clanton had put together during lunch.

Brett and Jason had stopped on their way home to lunch and had related the events of the morning to an attentive audience. Mr. Clanton had quickly rearranged the front page to insert a large headline, Derailed Train on Fisher Mountain. He knew that would sell many extra copies of the paper as had last week's headline Boy and Father Trapped.

Over five hundred copies were run by the time the printing ended in early afternoon. The first half of the run was folded and stacked. These were for local delivery. Earl and Adam put together pre-counted stacks for the station, the mill and larger businesses, and the Jenkins General Store. These and the single subscriber copies were loaded into the delivery wagon. It was a wet job as the rain beat down on the two workers. The fact that the wagon was backed up to the back door gave little protection because the wind was blowing hard and driving the water right into the shop. Adam got the payment book while Earl hitched up Tiffany, Mr. Clanton's bay mare. Earl then returned to the shop to help put together and label the bundles for delivery by train. Adam climbed onto the hooded wagon seat and set off for the local deliveries.

By four o'clock, Adam was back for the bundles to go out on the train. Earl and Mr. Clanton had them tied and labeled when the wagon arrived. Adam eased Tiffany up close to the board walkway at the front door. He set the brake, hopped down, and dashed for the shop entrance. The papers were quickly loaded. As the two men returned to clean up and close the office for the weekend, Adam set out down the street toward the station. Halting at the end of the platform on Main Street, he hitched the mare to a hitching post and ran across the wooden decking for the station door.

The main room of the station was an open area with a potbelly stove in the center and benches around the three outside walls. A counter ran across the room dividing the office area from the waiting room. A number of people were seated on benches talking with friends, reading the paper, or sleeping while they waited for the six o'clock train. At the counter a man was purchasing his ticket from the stationmaster, Mr. Coates. The purchase completed, the stationmaster turned toward Adam.

"Howdy, Adam," the tall thin-featured man greeted. "Ya lookin' for a baggage wagon?"

"Yes, sir," the boy replied. Mr. Coates took off his wire-rimmed glasses and rubbed an itchy eye. Settling the glasses in place again, he spoke. "Help yerself to the one just outside the baggage room, I'll send Jarrett over to the baggage car ta help ya load."

"Thanks, Mr. Coates." A stiff breeze blew in as the boy turned to the door to leave. "Good sign," he called back to the stationmaster.

"How so?"

"The storm may be blowin' itself out." Adam left.

The boy wheeled the baggage wagon over to the delivery wagon, transferred the newspapers, then pulled the load across to the baggage car at the end of the line of parked coaches. Jarrett, Mr. Coates' fourteen-year-old son, was waiting in the open doorway. The breeze blew his blond hair across his eyes making it difficult to see. Adam enjoyed the feel of the warm wind as it flapped at his shirt and whipped through his hair. The wind-driven rain had lessened to heavy drops splatting against his body and the side of the train car.

"Looks like it's lettin' up," Jarrett called over the noise of the wind. "Clouds are thinnin'."

"Be nice to see the sun again," the younger boy put in. "Hope it's clear for the Fourth."

Adam pulled himself onto the wagon bed. "Here comes!" he warned as the first bundle was hurled toward Jarrett. They loaded the papers quickly.

"Wait up," Jarrett said as he rolled the door closed. The door to the car's platform slammed as he hurried down the steps and caught up to Adam. The two of them pulled the wagon back to the baggage room and left it outside the door.

"Wanta stop for a cup o' chocolate?" Jarrett asked.

"Later," Adam replied. "I've gotta get the wagon back ta the Herald. I told Brett and Jason ta meet me there at five. We'll stop back ta see the train leave."

"See ya then." Jarrett turned in at the station door as Adam walked off toward the waiting Tiffany.

*   *   *

The rain had stopped by the time Adam, Brett, and Jason returned to the station. Jarrett and his father were both busy loading personal baggage onto the baggage wagon and making sure each item was properly ticketed toward its destination. Matt Kelton, a trainman on Jay's crew was helping load at the door of the baggage car, moving freight and small packages on board from another baggage wagon.

"This load's ready, Matt," the stationmaster called. The trainman pulled the empty wagon back to the freight room door.

"Need any help?" Adam asked as the trio walked across from the street.

"Jest in time," Jarrett replied as he set a leather travel bag on the load. At first there had been only a few people standing on the platform, but as train time drew closer, many who had been waiting inside came out. Others arrived from various points in town, having purchased tickets earlier or been occupied by other matters right up to the last moment. The boys maneuvered the baggage vehicle toward the open door of the car, weaving in and out of the growing crowd along the way. Mr. Kelton stayed close at hand in case they wanted help.

Conversation filled the air with a droning thickness combining with the damp heat which began to stagnate the air following the storm. The rain had stopped, the breeze had passed, the clouds were thinning. The early evening sun came out from under the clouds in a hot and hazy brightness.

The whistle sounded, the bell began to ring, and the sound of the engine steamed slowly toward the crowd from the yard, bringing an expectant hush. The boys finished emptying the freight wagon by handing the last piece of luggage through the door to Mr. Kelton. They drew the wagon back to its resting place. Number Twenty-One moved down the track behind the station, passed through the switch to the passing track, and backed up past the station. The locomotive paused just beyond the switch for the siding on which the train waited. Dan stepped down and threw the switch. He then stepped up onto the pilot of the engine which he rode to the end of the train. Since the first stop was back up the line five miles at Day's End, the train would be coupled to the front of the engine, which would back up to Day's End. Once in the station area of that first stop, it could use the pass track and move to the front of the train for the trip to Arlee. The train was together. The bell stopped ringing as the black smoke billowed quietly from the stack and the steam echoed in its chambers, pulsating like an irregular heartbeat.

"All aboard!" Dan shouted, "for stops at Day's End, Kingston, Blakesville, Arlee, and points north and south."

The people surged noisily toward the steps. The commotion subsided as the last of them climbed the steps to the two coaches.

"I'm goin' over ta see Jay a minute," Jason announced.

"I'll go with ya," Brett joined.

The two boys strolled over to the engine cab while Jarrett and Adam climbed up on the baggage wagon to watch. They stood on the bed leaning up against the end frame. In the engine cab, Scot noticed the boys first.

"Jay," Scot spoke, "Ya got company."

The engineer walked over to the top of the steps.

"How ya doin', boys," he greeted.

"Will ya see my folks tanight?" Jason asked.

"Plan ta," Jay replied.

"Tell them I said Hi and I'm havin a great time. Ask if I can stay an extra day for the Fourth and go home the fifth." Jason stood looking up toward the engineer with one hand on a grab iron for support.

"Now that's a whole lot for my memory to hold ta, but I'll do my best, Jason. See ya tomorrow, Brett. Time ta pull out."

Dan waved all clear as he stepped aboard the coach. Jay acknowledged with two short whistle blasts. Jarrett and Adam waved from their perch as they saw Jay look toward them. He waved back, then stepped across to the throttle. Scot set the bell to ringing as the train eased backwards out of the siding. It paused after clearing for Matt to throw the switch clear for the passing track. It paused again after clearing the switch for the main. Then Number Twenty-One picked up speed and rapidly disappeared into the woodlands on its way to Day's End. The b6ys watched the last of the smoke from its stack drift off and fade into the air.

The last echo of the pistons faded into the distance. "Come on in," Jarrett invited. "Ma's baked some fresh cookies. We can have some and wait for the run by."

"Sounds fine by me," Adam accepted. "Ya know, Little Brother, you've never seen Jay runnin' her wide open. She's a real beauty ta watch when she runs past full open."

Between the doors to the station and the freight room was the office hallway door. Just inside, a staircase led upstairs to the stationmaster's residence. The boys went up the steps two at a time. The door at the top stood open to allow a breeze to circulate. Entering the upper area, Jarrett led the way into the kitchen to the immediate right. A gangly girl of eight sat at the table playing with a stuffed doll and setting out eating utensils for dinner.

"Hi, Carry, Where's Ma?" Jarrett inquired.

"She's gone ta see if Pa's ready for supper," his sister replied as she laid out a place setting. She glanced up at the other boys. "Hi, Adam." Carry smiled. "Who's your friends?"

Adam introduced Brett and Jason. Mr. and Mrs. Coates came up from the office.

"Hi, boys," the stationmaster greeted.

"I bet Jarrett's brought ya up for cookies," Mrs. Coates guessed. Adam confirmed it. "Well, Jarrett, you get the cookie jar. Maybe your sister will pour some milk ta go with 'em while I get supper on. No more than two each. You'll spoil your appetites."

The boys stood out of the way by the drain board and munched on their snack and drank their milk while Mrs. Coates got supper ready for her family. The kitchen was quite warm from the heat of the stove and the thick sultry air following the storm.

"Jarrett," his mother spoke, "you can go down with your friends until the train goes by. We'll hold supper for you."

The boys went back down to the platform. After the noise and commotion leading up to the train's departure, the empty quiet seemed intense. A long fifteen minutes passed before they heard Twenty-One's whistle echo toward them.

"There she comes," Brett pointed to the plume of smoke racing through the trees. The chugging locomotive grew louder as it burst into view racing down the main. The whistle screamed proudly as the train roared deafeningly past in a majestic whirlwind of dust, cinders, steam, smoke, and clattering wheels. The boys squinted their eyes against the sudden rush of air and dirt as a streak of yellow and green and reflecting glass flashed by. The train and wind noise shrank into the distance and was gone.

"Wow!" Brett exclaimed.

"See what I mean," Adam commented.

"Yea," Jason said in admiration.

"Time for us ta head fer home," Adam interrupted. "See ya later, Jarrett."

"So long," Jarrett said as he turned toward the station office door.

Adam and his friends walked to the end of the platform. They stepped out onto Main Street and turned homeward.

THE FOURTH

The next several days were bright and sunny with temperatures rising into the eighties during the day and dropping to the low sixties at night. Jarrett took Jamie's place walking the track to Chambers Crossing during the weekend. Adam, Brett, and Jason went along Saturday. On Sunday the family was at church. A track crew took over during the week.

Most of the weekend was spent fishing, swimming, and exploring when there weren't farm chores to help with. Monday was back to regular work routine on the mountain and at the mill. Brett and Jason spent much of the day in town, at the company yard, or playing around the farm. Adam went with his father for the day. Tuesday, the three were together again spending the morning in the fields and riding the last train to South Camp and back. Jay brought word that Jason could stay the Fourth. His folks had decided that they would take a holiday trip and ride out on the morning train to spend the day. They had made arrangements to stay at the Railroad Hotel in Snow Shoe for the night and would take Jason back with them the following day.

A letter arrived from Mrs. Tompkins on Tuesday. She was quite upset about the accident and insisted that Brett and his father return to Baltimore where life was civilized and Brett would be safer. Brett pleaded with his father to let him stay and they both wrote back that they were doing fine and would be staying on as originally planned. Mr. Tompkins explained that they were in good care with Doc Blevins and that he was back to work and proceeding carefully. Brett wrote of his friend's visit and of the many things they were doing. He explained that he was very happy where he was, but he really wished his mother would come. He even expressed the hope that she, too, might like it there in Snow Shoe. He wished the whole family could move there to stay. The Johnstons arrived Friday morning. Adam stayed at home to help his mother fix picnic supper for the afternoon. Brett and Jason met Jason's parents at the station and went with them to check in at the hotel. The town was buzzing with activity. Bunting and streamers were hung from the store fronts. Flags were displayed up and down Railroad Avenue. A parade was planned for midday followed by games, activities, and contests in various locations during the afternoon. Firecrackers were popping all over town as children lit off explosive strings and tossed them at passersby or on the street or under a wagon. They delighted in seeing people or animals jump at the unexpected noise.

Following lunch in the hotel's dining room, Brett and his friend's family found a place on the wooden walkway out front to watch the festivities. A crowd began to form along either side of the street. The grown folk stood and talked and waited. The youngsters were busy running about and chasing each other.

"Where's your pa, Brett?" Mrs. Johnston asked. She craned her neck to look for Mr. Tompkins in the crowd.

Before the boy could answer, a sizzling string of small firecrackers landed on the walk nearby.

"Look out!" Brett warned. He moved away from the hissing bundle just as they began to pop and jump about. Quickly the crackling sparks and smoke subsided to a pile of ash.

Mr. Johnston put a reassuring hand on Brett's shoulder. "They're really quite harmless, Brett. They make more noise than anything else."

The crowd nearby shifted, then parted reluctantly to allow the Tylers and Mr. Tompkins to slip through.

"Good to see you again, Hank," Mr. Tompkins greeted, exchanging handshakes. "Hello, Nancy. I'd like you folks to meet the Tylers." Introductions were made as well as a report of plans for picnic supper back at the farm following the activities of the afternoon. The crowd stilled some. A barefoot boy ran out into the street excitedly, pointing toward the end of town.

"Here they come!" he shouted.

People strained forward for a better view. From up the avenue toward the logging company there came the tinny sound of a band. The music grew closer as a fireman's band marched down the dusty street. It was preceded by a Civil War Veterans' color guard and followed by the town fire equipment.

"Follow me!" Adam called to Brett and Jason.

He dashed into the hotel with the two close at his heels. Adam paused at the desk in the empty 1abby to check the register. Slipping behind the counter, he snatched a key from the board, then led the way to the second floor.

"This is your folk's room, Jason. It'll have a good view."

Adam unlocked the door. Quickly they crossed the room to a front window.

"How about the roof?" Jason suggested. The three boys climbed through the window to the roof over the sidewalk. It was flat and edged with a railing. The boys leaned over the rail and had a good view of the entire street.

The procession passed smartly with flags waving, drums rolling, and a fair rendition of the Battle Hymn and other lively marches. The army veterans looked handsome in their faded blue uniforms with sparkling brass buttons and colorful insignia and stripes. The band was dressed in red and black. Polished visors reflected the sun. The horses pranced smartly as they drew the shining, varnished fire wagons along the parade route.

The parade was followed by horse races which started in front of the bank, covered a two-block course around the center of town and finished at the starting line. Lumberjack contests were held in the mill yard with log rolling in the mill pond. There were sawing, axe cutting, and log splitting contests. Mr. Tyler entered several of these. He was dunked in the log rolling contest and placed second in the two-man saw contest with Lyle as his partner.

After the afternoon activities, the various families went their own ways for supper. The Johnston, Tyler, and Tompkins families gathered at the Tyler farm for a picnic in the back yard. That evening a great fireworks display was fired off from the middle of the tracks across from the station. It could be seen from anywhere in town and was a truly spectacular sight. Rockets of many colors burst, crackled, and exploded in the sky.

Jason spent his last night with Brett. His parents visited with Mr. Tompkins and the Tylers until late in the evening, then walked the three blocks back to the hotel to retire for the night. Before going to bed, the three boys went out in the back yard to look at the stars and to talk some. They sat on the porch steps.

"The sky's sure clear tonight," observed Adam.

Brett commented, "In Baltimore you don't much notice the stars. Smoke from the factories and light from so many houses sometimes makes it hard ta see."

"Look," pointed Jason. "There's a thin cloud goin' across the moon. Sure looks spooky."

"Did ya ever wonder if there's someone livin' out there?" Brett pondered.

"Sure is a mighty big space." Adam laid back against the steps. "You'd think it's possible."

They all rested against the steps and gazed at the vastness of the universe. A light breeze stirred and brushed across their faces. It flicked at shirt collars and wisps of hair.

"It's been a fun week," Brett said.

"Sure has," Jason added. "Thanks for invitin' me ta come. Seems like I been here a long time and suddenly I gotta go home."

"Maybe I can visit you before I have ta go back home," Brett suggested.

"You know," Adam offered, "it might be possible ta ride down with Jay on Friday and come back Saturday."

"Yeh, that's a neat idea," Brett beamed. "I'll hafta check with Pa."

The back door opened and Mrs. Johnston stepped out onto the porch. "Kinda nice out here," she spoke softly. "We're goin' now, Jason." Her son got up to give her a kiss good night. She added a quick hug. "Why not bring Brett and Adam over in the morning and have breakfast with us at the hotel," she suggested.

"What da ya guys think?" Jason asked.

"Okay," Adam accepted.

"See ya real early. The train leaves at six-thirty, so we haf ta eat at quarter til."

"We'll be there," said Brett.

"Fine. Good night, boys."

They bid her good night. The door squeaked open and clapped shut. Jason's mother was gone.

"We best turn in." Adam stood up stiffly as he spoke. They all stretched as they stood, then climbed the steps and let the door slam as they entered the house. Adam and Brett said good night to their parents and told them they were getting up early to go with Jason and have breakfast with his family.

Adam said good night to his friends at the top of the stairs and headed for his room. Jason and Brett got ready for bed, then took one last look out the window together toward the dark shape of the mountain.

"It's sure been an exciting week," Jason said. "I'm not ever gonna' forget it."

They climbed into their beds and lay awake a short time longer. Exhaustion overtook them and they drifted off to sleep.

*   *   *

The sky was still dark. Stars winked brightly in the inky blackness. The moon had long since dipped below the western horizon and a thin band of gold had begun to stretch across the eastern horizon. The boys walked quietly along the dark street. The silhouettes of houses loomed dark and quiet along either side. Their footfalls echoed on the wooden walk as the boys approached the business district. They reached the brightly lighted hotel and entered a busy lobby. Several people were bringing their luggage down and setting it near the counter. The boys looked up and saw Mr. Johnston.

"Mornin', boys," Jason's pa greeted as he descended the staircase, luggage in hand. He set the bags beside a chair in the lobby.

The boys followed him through the archway into the dining room. Breakfast consisted of the hotel's traditional bacon and eggs, home-fried potatoes, biscuits, and hot cakes. Adam, Brett, and the Johnstons talked of the past week's adventures as they ate. When finished, Mr. Johnston excused himself to settle the bill. The others joined him in the lobby. Then they departed and walked across the street to the station.

Since the fourth had fallen on Friday, a special holiday schedule had been activated. Workers had left for the weekend on a Thursday night train which stayed over in Arlee and Friday morning's run was a holiday special. There was no Friday night train, instead, a special run was scheduled for Saturday morning. Jason's family would be on this train.

The train had already pulled into the station and stood ready to depart. Having just come from Day's End, it was setting on the main, ready to leave directly for Arlee. The boys exchanged farewells. Brett was informed that he had an open invitation to come to Arlee whenever he could.

Jason embraced his friend. "So long, Brett," he said. "You and Adam tell your folks thanks."

"So long, Brett," Mr. Johnston offered his hand.

Jason's mother parted with a light kiss on his cheek. "Bye, Adam." Adam, too, received the same honors.

Jason and his parents climbed aboard. Mr. Seegers waved all aboard. He paused momentarily to acknowledge Brett and Adam, then stepped up to the coach platform as the train pulled out. The Johnstons waved from the window. They were soon lost from view as the train quickly picked up speed and left the station. Brett and Adam waited until it was out of sight, then turned and started back toward the house.

*   *   *

The days passed quickly. The following week Mr. Tompkins was back on the mountain. Brett talked to his father about his earlier wish to find something he could do so that he, too, could work part time at South Camp. Horace welcomed Brett's help around the kitchen. The boy would go up on the mid-day run and spend the afternoon at the logging camp returning on the last train with his father. Sometimes he went up on the morning train and stayed the day.

As his ribs mended, Brett began to try his hand at a greater variety of jobs. Most of the men welcomed his presence. Over the course of the next weeks he learned most of the operation that went on in the logging camp. He rode the engine much of the time and began to learn how to operate it under Jay and Scot's watchful teaching. Soon he was tending the fire, checking gauges, and taking turns at the throttle. At the camp he learned to operate the loader and to tie on guide lines. The boy was taught how to handle an ax, a two-man saw, and a drag team. He cared for the horses and worked in the mess tent. Brett developed strength he didn't know he had, but learned, too, there was much he couldn't do because he wasn't grown enough to have the greater strength needed for the heavier work. Midway through July, Brett got a chance to take the Friday run to Arlee and spend the night with Jason. While in Arlee, he explored the town, and enjoyed riding with the yard crew in the train yards and the engine facility. The visit was brief as he had to return on Saturday with the morning run back to Snow Shoe.

Mrs. Tompkins wrote to say that she was at first upset by his father's decision not to return to Baltimore. But she appreciated Brett's news about the fun he was having and the experiences and adventure he was enjoying. She could understand the decision to stay and felt better knowing he was recovering from his injuries and gaining in strength. Brett again wrote, sharing his latest experiences and expressing his wish that his mother would join them in Snow Shoe or at least come to visit.

Summer heat set in as a dry spell hung on during the middle of July. The days of hot sun and the cool dry nights stretched on toward the end of the month. Brett had fully mended and his father had shed his cast and crutches. He, too, was nearly finished mending. The last week of July had begun. Brett had just returned from a full weekend in Arlee. His father had given him the wonderful news that his mother had written to say that she expected to come up from Baltimore by the end of the week. She had been thinking about Brett's letters and decided that maybe she should visit to see what it was that made him so happy so far from home. Mrs. Tompkins planned to arrive on the Friday train.

OVERNIGHT
ON THE MOUNTAIN

The afternoon sun glared down on the canvas of the mess tent radiating a stuffy heat underneath. No breeze offered any relief in the ninety degree air. Brett's hair was streaked with sweat and lay wet and sticky against his forehead and the back of his neck. Rivulets of perspiration ran down his cheeks and dripped from his chin. The boy's light-weight cotton shirt stuck wet against his back.

Brett lay the rolling pin down on the plank table and picked up the round tin cutter. Pushing the metal lightly into the bowl of flour, he knocked it against the side and began cutting biscuits. His sweaty hands were caked with flour and his face had streaks of white where he'd wiped the back of his hand to remove excesses of moisture. The boy laid the cutter aside. Carefully lifting the edges of dough, he dropped the cuttings in a pile near the edge of the board. Then he placed the fresh cut biscuits in neat rows on a freshly greased baking sheet. Once the board was cleared, the cuttings were kneaded into a ball of dough and rolled again into a sheet about a half-inch thick. The cutting, rolling, and cutting was repeated until the last of the dough was consumed. When finished, the dough had gone into just over four dozen biscuits.

"This batch is ready," Brett announced. He picked up two of the tin sheets, carried them to the kitchen tent, and set them on a work table where several others had already been lined up.

"That's the last of it," Horace informed. He finished turning chicken parts and shoved the pan back into the oven. The cook straightened up and turned toward the boy. Sweat dripped from his face and arms as he picked up a towel to mop his face and wipe his hands.

For just a brief moment the boy studied the grizzled face of the old man, then left to bring the remaining sheets of biscuits. He had come to know the cook quite well. He had learned that the cook had once worked for his grandfather. A serious logging accident had crushed his left leg leaving him with a bad limp. While he seemed gruff and sharp with people, he was really a kind man. The two of them had become fair friends during the past month and he had taught Brett a lot about preparing and cooking food. The boy placed the last of the sheets on the table and cleaned up his work area. He stepped outside the work area to pour some water into a wash basin and to clean off the flour and dough that had caked on his hands. Dumping the water, Brett returned and sat on a vegetable crate near the table. The cook was stirring a large pot of cut beans.

Light footsteps entered the mess tent. Brett turned and saw Adam headed toward the kitchen. He looked exhausted.

"Boy, am I tired." Adam plopped down on a nearby bench. "I'll sleep well tonight."

"What were ya doin' this afternoon?" Brett asked.

Adam opened his shirt and pulled the shirt tail around to wipe his face. Then he explained, "Been working with Toby's team, draggin'" The older boy got up, walked over to the water bucket and dipped out a dipperful. He drank half of it and poured the rest over his head. "See ya later," Adam commented as he started to leave again. "Nearly time to put up the team for the night."

As if to confirm this, the "Scott's" whistle announced its arrival.

Brett spoke, "Mr. Leeds, I'll be over watchin Jay change over trains."

"Set up when ya get back." Horace watched a moment as the boy left, and gazed beyond to see the train arriving.

Monday's work drew to a close as the crews came in and hung their tools up on racks on the outside walls of the bunk cars. The teamsters brought their teams in, turned them loose in the corral, and stowed their harnesses in the tack shed. The earlier quiet of the afternoon gave way to the general commotion of cleaning up and gathering for supper. Brett had returned to set out the tables. The train had been changed over and the last load was on its way to the mill. Brett and Adam and their fathers were staying over. Mr. Tompkins had decided that they were both in good health now and knew that his son had been pulling his workload and was enjoying his experiences with the company operation. The four of them sat together for supper and shared the day's activities with each other.

After supper Adam helped Brett with his cleanup chores. The men sat around telling stories and sharpening their tools. The boys joined when the last of the supper dishes had been put away.

"Hey, Brett," Lyle called. "Did ya ever hear the story of Paul Bunyan?"

"Who's he?" Brett took interest.

"Why only the greatest lumber man who ever lived!" Sean added.

"Horace," Mr. Tyler spoke. "You know the story best. Why, as I recall, you even worked with ole Paul once."

"Yep," Horace began. His face lit up in a way Brett had never before seen as he commenced his story. "I met ole Paul while working in a camp out in Washington state back in the summer of forty-eight. He and Blue, that's his big ox, were passin' through and stayed ta work the summer."

Brett was entranced by the story. Everyone else stopped what he was doing to listen again to a story they'd heard before, but never tired of. The evening drifted on lazily as the men joined together in song and story. Darkness moved in slowly as the sun settled toward the horizon. Sharpening stones and files were put away and tools hung in their places as the men spread out their bedrolls. Nobody slept in the bunk cars during the hot season. Instead, most settled on the ground in front, or under the canvas covering of the mess tent.

Adam and Brett picked up their blankets from the storage area of the supply tent and began to hunt a place to spread them. They settled on a spot between the mess tent and the corral where they'd have a clear view of the sky and the stars. Adam checked the ground for any twigs or stones that would cause discomfort and tossed them aside. He instructed Brett on how to clear the ground and Brett joined in to help. Two blankets were laid down over a layer of grasses pulled from outside the corral enclosure and a third was folded to provide a make-shift pillow.

Brett sat down on the blankets. "Seems quite hard," he observed.

"It takes gettin' used ta," Adam agreed. "The men from the crews have straw mattresses from their bunks and use them ta sleep on. Ya gotta agree, this sure is different."

"Sure is." Brett took his shoes off and set them on the ground near his head. Adam did likewise.

A light whinnying and rustlings from the corral indicated some of the horses were up and about. Quiet movement and subdued conversation hung in the air from several directions as the men settled in their bedrolls. Twilight slipped silently into darkness as the red glow on the western horizon faded into a rich, deep blue which was reaching across from the east. The horses settled quietly. The conversation from the various dark silhouettes scattered about, drifted into soft snoring as the dark shapes settled into prone shadows. The boys continued to talk quietly as the night noises of the tree toads and crickets blended with the sounds of sleeping men.

"We musta dragged in a dozen logs in two hours," Adam was saying.

"I never cut so many biscuits or seen so many set out at a single time," Brett added.

"You sure musta looked a sight with all that flour," Adam laughed quietly.

"Not much worse than you with all that water runnin' off your head." Brett, too, laughed lightly. He lay on his back and gazed at the sparkling starlit sky. "Sure is pretty."

"If ya look through the trees," Adam pointed, "the moon is comin' up."

The large, pale, bright disk glowed through the trees casting strange shadows about the field.

"See ya in the mornin'," Adam yawned. He stretched out on the blanket, then curled into a comfortable position. Sleep came quickly.

Brett sat up and gazed at the nighttime landscape. The familiar shapes by day had become dark shadows which seemed to move and breathe in the moonlight. Brett felt uneasy with this and decided to lie back down. He was tired and felt ready to sleep. As the moon climbed above the treetops, the boy slipped into slumber and dreamed of Friday and his mother's arrival from Baltimore.

*   *   *

Brett became aware of someone shaking him and calling his name.

"Brett, wake up." It was Adam.

The boy rolled over on his back and forced his eyes open. He felt drained of energy and so tired. If only he could ignore his friend and just go back to sleep. Brett stretched hard, tensing his arms and yawning. He rubbed his eyes with the heels of his hands.

"What time is it?" he asked sleepily.

"Seven, Little Brother. Breakfast is on. Ya better hurry if ya wanta eat."

Brett lay there a minute trying to make his mind come clear so he could decide what to do next. He reached back over his head for his shoes. Finding them, he pulled them down to the blanket beside him. The boy sat up, paused a moment, then dragged his feet up and put his shoes on. Adam had begun to fold the blankets. Securing the last knot in his laces, Brett stood up and helped fold the last blanket.

The sun was already well clear of the horizon and driving away the cool night air with a radiating heat that warmed all it touched. The sky was a clear bright blue with no sign of clouds. The greens and browns of the woodland landscape were rich in color. Sparrows and starlings chattered in the trees and underbrush and the crows cawed in the distance, disturbed by the bustle of the camp. The crew was already gathered in the mess tent consuming platefuls of eggs, bacon, and biscuits. The boys returned from putting away their blankets and found empty places for them near the end of the tables. The aromas of breakfast caught them and awakened their appetites.

The boys remained to help clean up as the men left to begin work on the morning load.

"Adam," Brett asked, "Who does this work when we're not here?"

"Each crew takes a turn supplying help," the older boy explained as he gathered the forks onto a plate. "It usually works out that each man has one duty day a month."

The table boards were cleared and the dishes washed up. While the boys were occupied with kitchen duty, the crew was busy firing up the boiler for the loader. The air came alive with the sounds of axes and saws biting into tree trunks on the distant hilltops. The crash of falling trees soon joined the chorus. A hissing sound of rushing steam in the loader was soon punctuated by the churning of its pistons as the machinery was slipped into operation. Black smoke boiled from the stack as the boom and hook swung into motion. The boys watched the start up through the open sides of the kitchen tent. When finished with cleanup, they left to help with work at the loader.

The loader stood on a short siding beside the log cars. A flatcar with board sides was coupled behind and served as a large woodbin from which the fire box of the steam boiler was fed. The steam-powered winch eased out line as the operator dropped the hook toward a tree section which had been dragged in from the slope. The cable was fed around the log and attached to the hook. Guide lines were secured. A ground crew worked the guide lines as the winch raised the log from the ground. The boom was swung over the flat and the log lowered into the load. Adam and Brett scrambled onto the flat to disconnect the hook and throw off the guide lines. Their presence wasn't needed as one of the ground crew usually did the job. But the help the boys provided always made the job go faster.

As the morning wore on and the sun's heat became more intense, the crew stripped off their shirts. They had become completely soaked with sweat to the point where their sticky weight got in the way.

Brett and Adam stood back along the side of the load holding onto the upright stakes for support as the boom swung its load overhead. Marc Brenner and Andrew Breuers guided the ends swinging the log parallel to the flat. As it was lowered into place, the boys moved in and untied the guide ropes. The cable around the center went slack as the hook dropped. Adam slipped the top loop off the hook and waved "all clear." The hook rose, pulling the cable from under the log and rolling the log across the load away from the boys.

When the first car was finished being loaded, the group paused for a rest.

"Time to begin water rounds," Adam announced.

"On my way," Brett replied. He climbed down, picked up his shirt from where it had been draped across the end coupler, and strolled over toward the mess tent.

Horace had already hitched the wagon, lashed on the water barrels, and filled them with fresh water. Brett threw his shirt across the wagon seat and climbed aboard. Taking up the reins, he waved to Horace as he clicked the horses into motion. The wagon rumbled off on its rounds to the crews working on the slopes. Brett stopped at each work area to wait while the men gathered around the wagon to take turns with the tin water cups.

Mr. Tompkins strolled up to the wagon at one of its stops. "You look tired, son," he observed as he sipped the water.

"I had a hard time gettin' up this mornin'. But I feel much better now, Pa." Brett smiled a tired smile.

"Just the same, Mr. Tyler and I want you both to go down on the morning load. Have dinner at the house and go to bed a while. You don't want to be sick when your mother arrives."

"No, sir, I surely don't. But can't I jest stay the day and go ta bed early tonight?"

"No, son. You're too tired."

"Yes, Sir," Brett moaned. He continued his rounds, finishing with the loader crew. Eight cars were finished and the last two just begun as the "Scott" pulled in. Mr. Tyler was present to receive the mail bags. There was nothing else to unload since all supplies were delivered on the Friday runs. The engine crew took a break while the last load was completed. Brett returned the wagon to Horace who unhitched the team and tied the horses to a tree in the shade until it was time for the afternoon rounds. Brett put out water buckets for each of the horses.

A short time later, Adam joined his friend in the kitchen area to report that the load was complete and it was time to leave. Brett found the cook.

"Mr. Leeds, Pa says I'm to go down with the load. See ya tomorrow maybe."

"See ya then," Horace said as he bent over the work table.

Brett paused, but the man never turned around.

"Come on, Little Brother. The train's ready. And don't forget yer shirt."

Brett picked up his shirt and slipped it on as they walked toward the train. Horace turned to watch them leave, but resumed his work when he saw Brett pause to look back.

After another five minutes, the "Scott" sounded its whistle for noon break, then slid into motion as it began its run back to the mill.

ORDEAL BY FIRE

The movement of the train stirred up a refreshing breeze across the open platform of the caboose. Brett's shirt flapped lightly in the moving air stream. His sweaty trousers and the back of his shirt clung to his flesh and felt coolingly refreshing as the air seeped through them. He and Adam watched the quiet forest slip past. Adam looked up and watched the smoke from the engine's stack billow past and diffuse into the air. Beyond the smoke and treetops, patches of blue sky spread its covering. Rays of sunlight poured through holes in the leafy canopy, casting dancing columns of brightness throughout the woodland.

In the distance could be heard the frantic calling of a crow. It was soon taken up by a small chorus.

"Look!" Brett pointed. "Deer! Several of them!"

Adam saw them, too.

"Something's wrong. They're running scared."

The noise of the crows became intense and seemed to fill the air.

A number of small animals ran past as several birds took to the air. Adam looked toward the front of the train. A look of amazement passed across his face and was quickly replaced by a mixture of awe and fear. Brett followed his gaze and saw a dark cloud rising through the trees and hanging in the air above the forest.

"Smoke?" he asked.

"Forest fire," Adam confirmed. "It's just ahead. I'm not sure how far or just where. But from the look of it, it's bound ta be big."

The train slowed to a stop as the fireman sounded three short blasts on the whistle. Mr. Jackson and Mr. Wetherby ran forward from the last log load. The boys followed close behind. They could detect the roar of a huge blaze in the distance beyond the growing wave of smoke.

"What da ya think?" Mr. Jackson asked, "Shall we go back ta the camp?"

Mr. Leary replied, "If there's a chance ta get through, we best go on inta Snow Shoe and pick up the fire train. Everyone ride up front here, so we know where each other is."

The black wave thickened and rose higher about a quarter of a mile ahead. It didn't seem to make any move except to enlarge itself. The engineer eased the throttle forward and the train began to move. As it approached the blackness, the wave rose up, crested, then rolled swiftly over them. They choked in its acrid thickness as it poured into their lungs and burned.

"Get down!" Mr. Bond yelled. "Get down on the floor!"

The boys and the crewmen dropped to the floor of the cab. Less smoke hung near the floor and they were able to catch their breath. Mr. Leary opened the throttle some and let the engine run itself as he ducked down for air. The roar of the fire grew closer. Crackling flames were distinctly audible. The blackness took on a red glow as it began to lift to a canopy hovering just above the roof line.

Brett and Adam stood up cautiously.

"Climb up on my box." Mr. Bond indicated the area near the fireman's seat.

The boys crawled up onto the raised seat area and looked out at the eerie red twilight. The thick, black layer cut off all sight of the sky and the upper parts of the trees, and locked in an intensifying atmosphere of dry heat. A living red horizon danced in front of the moving rain, covering the forest world from side to side.

"Let's go back!" Mr. Wetherby shouted over the roar of the flames.

Mr. Bond pointed toward the rear of the train. "We're cut off! The fire's racing down the slope and has jumped the tracks!"

The roar of the blaze rose to a deafening crescendo as it suddenly swept over the train. The occupants of the engine were speechless with awe and stark fear. The heat was of such magnitude that one could neither imagine nor describe it. The air shimmered and danced with the living red monster and a myriad of naked shadows of trees disintegrating in the inferno. Fiery whirlwinds whipped around the engine. The caboose and loaded flatcars exploded into flame. The top of the tender load also ignited. Brett felt as if he too would burst into flames any minute. Pain flooded his lungs and wrapped his body as dizziness came over him. He felt Adam pulling him down to the floor under the window opening, then lay his body over Brett's. It was like a dream. The crewmen dropped like melting wax. A wave of unconsciousness swept over the boy washing him in cooling relief.

Within minutes, the fiery train passed from the blazing inferno into a world of charred corpses standing sizzling as smoke rose in wispy silence. As the clearer air blew through the cab and the roar of the fire slipped away, the younger boy became aware of the rumbling vibrations of the moving engine. The heat was gone. Had he dreamed it? No, there was a body pressed close to his. Brett pushed himself up and clear of Adam. Adam's face was black with smoke, and his hair and clothes were singed from the heat. Brett shook him by the shoulders.

"Adam! Adam! Wake up!" he screamed. "Adam, can you hear me?" The older boy stirred. He opened his eyes and gazed at Brett with a blank stare. "Adam?" Brett asked, "are you all right?"

He knelt beside his friend. Adam's eyes were not focusing. He was moving some, as though trying to wake up from a deep sleep. The train jarred across a rough track connection. One of the bodies on the cab floor began to stir. Brett realized that no one was operating the locomotive. He stood up to look around and saw for the first time the blazing cars streaming fire behind. He saw, too, that the wood on the top of the tender load was burning, and suddenly realized the upper part of the engine's cab was gone leaving a charred remains from the window sills up. Brett glanced out the front to find out where they were. There was no front. The front of the cab had burned away leaving only a charred frame sitting across the boiler. Judging by the terrain, the switchback was less than a mile ahead.

Brett looked in the fire box to see if there was enough fuel for awhile. Then he carefully crossed the cab to the engineer's seat and eased back on the throttle, slowing the train to a safer speed for crossing the switch. Adam stirred again and pulled himself into a sitting position.

"You all right?" Brett called. He climbed down from his perch.

"I think so," Adam replied somewhat faintly. "A bit dizzy. Where is everyone?"

"On the floor."

There was movement from the floor as Mr. Wetherby pulled himself up. Adam and Brett knelt beside the crewmen to check on each. Mr. Leary had burns on his face, hands, and arms. His shirt was nearly burned off. He remained unconscious. The boys did not move him. Mr. Bond, too, was burned on his face and hands, but not as badly. His clothing was burned in spots and badly singed. Mr. Wetherby helped Mr. Jackson to a sitting position and braced him against the fireman's box. He was still dazed. Adam found it painful to move.

"Hey, Little Brother," he said, "Check my back. It hurts somethin' fierce."

When Adam turned around, Brett saw that the back of his friend's shirt was charred and sticky from fluid oozing from Adam's skin.

"It looks pretty bad," Brett informed his friend. "Ya better not lean against anything'."

Mr. Wetherby looked up from where he knelt by the engine's crew. "You boys all right?" he asked.

"I think so," Adam replied. "And you?"

"I'm a bit dizzy, yet. Dave is comin' around. Bob and Stewart look pretty bad."

"We're on fire," Brett stated.

Mr. Wetherby jumped up and looked behind the engine.

"Oh, my God!" he gasped.

Brett glanced out the front. They were approaching the switch. He climbed back up on the seat and slowed the train.

"Can you get the switch, Mr. Wetherby?" he asked.

The trainman moved cautiously to the steps. Brett stopped the train past the switch as Mr. Wetherby climbed down to throw over the points. As the train stood still, the flames settled to a less intense level of burning. In the wake of the train's passing, new fires had been set in the parts of the forest where the original fire had not yet burned. Mr. Wetherby climbed back up to the cab.

"What are we goin' ta do?" Adam asked. "We're gonna set fire to the valley all the way back ta Snow Shoe!"

There was a crackling and crushing sound as the caboose's roof and walls collapsed in a shower of sparks and embers.

"The log loads have dropped," Mr. Wetherby announced. "The stakes must have burned through back a ways allowing the loads to roll off. If we go carefully, what's left'll hold till we get nearer the creek. Then we can use the rake and push the larger pieces into the water."

There was a moan from the floor as the engineer began to stir. Mr. Jackson regained consciousness and drew himself onto his hands and knees.

"Buddy," the trainman called weakly, "help me up. Can't breathe too well yet. Get me by a window."

Brett glanced at the gauges as Mr. Wetherby helped the other man to the fireman's box.

"We need more fuel," the boy announced.

Adam moved toward the tender. He picked up the fire rake and pushed the burning and smoldering pieces from the top of the load. Then he drew down several pieces which he passed to Brett and Mr. Wetherby who threw them into the firebox. Brett shoved the shift lever into reverse and eased the throttle in. The train started moving.

"Let's try the whistle," Adam suggested. "Maybe they'll hear it in Snow Shoe and send some help."

"Good idea," Mr. Jackson said. He reached for the cord, but it was gone with the cab roof, and the whistle lever stood bare against the sky without a cord.

"Is there any rope in the seats?" Brett asked.

Mr. Wetherby rummaged through the fireman's box while Brett checked the engineer's box.

"Here's a piece," the man announced.

"Boost me up and I'll tie it on," Adam offered.

Mr. Wetherby helped Adam up onto the engineer's seat and balanced him there while the boy reached up to tie the cord onto the whistle.

"Got it," the boy called as he backed down carefully.

Brett slowed the train to a stop along the creek bank as Mr. Wetherby helped Adam back down off the seat to the floor.

"Dave, you feel up ta some work?" Mr. Wetherby asked.

"I'm ready," came the reply.

"You boys stay here while Dave an me see what we can clear," Mr. Wetherby instructed. "Adam, why don't you start on the whistle."

Adam started sounding the whistle in long wailing groups of three. The mournful shrieks echoed along the valley. Mr. Leary and Mr. Bond began to stir. Brett climbed down to see if they were conscious.

"What happened?" Mr. Leary groaned.

"We've been through the fire," Brett answered. "We're on our way back to town."

Adam stooped down. "Mr. Jackson and Mr. Wetherby are out back. They'll be finished shortly. You're burned pretty bad. Ya best stay put till we get the Doc."

A cloud of steam hissed into the air from the creek as a number of burning pieces of car bodies splashed into the water. The constant sound of splashing and hissing hung on the air for several minutes until the worst of the material was cleared.

The other two men climbed back aboard. "Not much left," Mr. Jackson announced.

"What're ya talkin' about?" the engineer asked.

"Most of the train's burned up," Adam explained.

Mr. Leary started to push himself up only to find that the painful burns on his hands couldn't withstand the pressure.

"Careful," Mr. Jackson warned. He helped the engineer to his feet. Mr. Leary winced with pain as he used his elbows for balance. "You best set up on your box and take it easy," the trainman suggested. He helped Mr. Leary to his seat and guided him into a braced sitting position where he could use his elbows for balance.

The fireman tried to pick himself up, stiffened in pain, and settled back to the floor.

"Let me help ya, Stewart," Mr. Wetherby offered.

He helped the injured man onto the fireman's box.

"Let's go," Mr. Jackson stated.

Brett eased in the throttle and the engine began to push the charred remains of the train toward the yards. Adam continued to sound the whistle.

"Yer doin' a fine job," Mr. Wetherby praised. "Jay taught ya well."

The two men gazed about them in amazement at the open space where the engine's cab used to be.

The train continued along the Stewart Creek valley for about fifteen minutes. As it left the slope of the mountain and provided a view of its face, the boys and crew could see that the fire was moving up toward the summit of the mountain. A large, black cloud blanketed the face of the mountain edged by several blackened areas where the fire had already passed. A second smaller fire area was visible where the blazing train had dropped burning debris along its passage from the main fire. The fire had intensified greatly over the past hour, and it was obvious that everyone for miles around must be aware of it by now and be preparing to fight it.

The train was still a quarter mile out from the yards when the boys and the men heard the call of another whistle. Adam ceased pulling the whistle cord and they all listened.

"That's Scot sounding Number Twenty-One," Mr. Leary stated.

"Can ya tell where they are?" Adam asked.

Mr. Jackson climbed onto the tender tank. "I can see their smoke," he called. "They're right behind us."

"Stop here, Brett," Mr. Leary instructed. "Adam, sound a short set of three, then stop. They'll see our smoke. Dave, put on some more wood."

The train screeched to a halt. It sat there, a scorched locomotive with ten burned-out flatcar frames and the remains of the caboose simmering at its rear. Mr. Jackson passed down more wood to Adam and Mr. Wetherby. Adam raked the fire down, then threw on the fresh fuel. They all watched as the column of smoke advanced through the trees. It rounded the last bend and the locomotive broke into view. Two short whistle blasts announced that the crew on Twenty-One had seen the logging train. Jay brought his engine up and stopped a few feet back. Coupled behind was the company mixed and the fire train. Several men stepped down from the coach to gawk at the smoking skeleton that stood on the tracks ahead. Jay and Dan ran forward to the "Scott". They quickly scrambled aboard to assess the situation.

"Boy are we glad ta see you!" Mr. Jackson exclaimed.

"You should o' seen it!" Brett cut in. "I never saw anythin' like it in my life. There was …"

"Hold on," Jay interrupted. "We've got ta get you tended and this train off the line so we can go after that fire."

"Jay," Mr. Leary spoke. "Stewart and I aren't too good. The boys and Buddy and Dave here did a fine job o' getting' us down. Better get Doc ta check Adam, though. His back doesn't look any too healthy."

Adam had been standing near the fire box. He suddenly grabbed at the gauges for support as his legs gave out from under.

"What's wrong?" Mr. Jackson stepped forward quickly to steady the boy.

"I lost my balance," Adam explained. "I'm kinda dizzy feelin'."

"Let yerself go. I got ya." Mr. Jackson helped Adam to the raised area in front of the fireman's seat. The boy's skin had become pale and clammy.

"I don't feel good," Adam complained. He knelt on the floor and gripped the charred window ledge for support.

Jay gave instructions. "I'm goin' ta clear onta the yard track. Buddy, get this train ta the station and park it. Then see that everyone gets ta Doc for tendin'. We'll go ahead up the mountain. You and Dave can move inta the yard after everyone's cared for. We'll tend the train later."

The engineer climbed back down and walked back to his train. Dan paused a moment before departing.

"You fellas take care now." He turned and left. Three short blasts from Twenty-One's whistle signaled its move.

"I'll take it from here, Brett," Mr. Wetherby said. "You look ta Adam."

Brett climbed down and crossed to the fireman's box. He sat on the floorboards by his friend and braced himself to support Adam. The "Scott" followed the other train down the track and paused above the switch while the other train cleared into the yard. Then Mr. Wetherby moved on down to the station area. Brett watched as Twenty-One's smoke marked its movement up the valley toward the mountain. He glanced once more at the black cloud hovering over the mountaintop and knew that the fire would soon be brought to an end.

The brakes squealed as the train slowed to a stop beside the station. The ordeal was over. It was now a matter of time until those who had been injured would be cared for. A small crowd of curious spectators gathered to stare at the strange sight of charred and smoking remains. Mr. Jackson climbed down to send for aid. Jarrett had come out from the station when the train arrived and was sent to fetch Doc Blevins. Mr. Coates came aboard to help the trainmen lower the engineer and the fireman to the platform. They were assisted to a nearby bench where they sat down to rest. Adam was helped down from the cab. Until now he'd been too busy to be aware of his burns. The constant seeping of body fluids had weakened him. The boy was becoming faint and began to drift into unconsciousness. He was assisted to a nearby baggage wagon and laid face down to rest. Brett stayed by his friend.

"Will he be all right, Mr. Jackson?" the boy asked.

"1 think so," the trainman answered. "He's played out and needs some rest."

"Hey, Little Brother," Adam whispered. "I'm jest tired. You let ole Doc to me and I'll be fine."

The older boy rested his head on his arm and relaxed.

"Mr. Jackson!" Brett panicked.

"He's okay," the man reassured. "He's just restin'."

Commotion at the edge of the gathering crowd announced the doctor's arrival. Doc Blevins worked his way through the spectators. Soon gentle hands were probing the charred and sticky scraps of cloth and flesh on Adam's back which, until this time, had gone unnoticed as nothing more than smoke and soot. Brett looked questioningly at the doctor for a verdict.

"He'll mend a lot faster than you did," the man assured. "It looks a lot worse than it really is. The burns are not deep and in three weeks will look more 1ike a bad case of sunburn."

Tears of relief welled up in Brett's eyes. Doc Blevins laid a consoling hand on the boy's sooty hair, Brett hugged the man and, burying his dirty face in the clean white shirt, wept briefly and uncontrollably. The doctor held the boy close, patting his shoulder gently. The boy caught his breath again and looked up at the kind, wrinkled face.

"Thanks, Doc." He smiled a teary smile. "Thanks."

Mr. Leary and Mr. Bond, like Adam, had suffered painful burns where they had been exposed to the tremendous heat of the fire. But the train had passed so quickly through the inferno that most were searing burns of the surface of the flesh. Wrappings and ointments would ease the pain and help the healing process. All had suffered some internal injury from breathing the hot air and smoke, but Brett and the other crewmen got off with minor burns and discomfort because they had been down low and away from the worst of the fire.

It took a day and a half to bring the fire under control. Crews worked around the clock cutting firebreaks, setting backfires, and pumping water along the railroad right-of-way. By midnight on Wednesday, the slope of the mountain had been reduced to a twinkling red glow. Brett and Adam sat up and watched from Brett's bedroom window as red coals winked in the glow of the moonlight. They hoped their fathers would soon be home. Eventually they tired of waiting and fell asleep on Brett's bed.

THE LONG-AWAITED VISIT

The morning sun rose hot and bright. Wisps of clouds drifted across the clear blue sky. From the blackened acres, of fire-scarred timberland light columns of white smoke drifted skyward. Warm rays of sunlight drifted through the open window setting off columns of dancing dust particles. A light breeze stirred the curtains and gently brushed loose strands of hair as it caressed the faces of the sleeping boys.

A door opened and closed downstairs. Excited, but quiet voices drifted up from below. The exhausted pair slept on. After a short time, stealthy footsteps mounted the stairs and stopped at the door. Carefully and quietly the door was opened and Mrs. Tyler peered in. She turned to someone waiting in the hall.

"They're still asleep," she whispered. The door closed softly. The footsteps retreated back downstairs.

In the kitchen Mr. Tyler and Mr. Tompkins spoke briefly of the battle to fight the fire. They were tired and hungry, having been gone since Monday morning. Mrs. Tyler told what she had learned of the boys' ordeal. The men ate a hearty breakfast, bathed at the well, and changed into clean clothes. They felt much better and told Mrs. Tyler to go ahead and wake the boys. They had missed their sons and were concerned when they heard of the train's fiery trip.

Adam and Brett didn't even wait to dress. They came down to the kitchen in their nightshirts even before Mrs. Tyler returned.

"Pa!" each greeted in unison. They flung themselves into their fathers' outstretched arms. Hugs were exchanged as each held the other in loving thankfulness that they were together again and safe. Mr. Tyler was careful to avoid touching Adam's back. They stood back to look at each other, then shared one more quick embrace.

"You boys hungry?" Mrs. Tyler asked as she entered the room.

"Starved," Brett answered.

"We thought you'd be home last night," Adam stated. "The fire seemed out by supper."

"We had to watch for flare-ups," Mr. Tompkins explained.

"Several times the fire restarted in places," continued Mr. Tyler. "Crews were stationed all around the edge to put out these hot spots."

The men described how the fire was fought and finally brought under control. The boys listened intently as they ate their breakfast. Then they shared the ordeal they'd experienced with their awe-struck fathers. It was so good to be together again and to see and talk to each other.

The noon hour approached. Mr. Tyler and Mr. Tompkins excused themselves to go to bed and get some rest. They had become very drowsy and unable to stay awake any longer. Brett and Adam went up to get dressed. They planned to go over to the company yard and see what was happening to the train. They also wanted to see what else was going on. All activity since the fire had started had been altered that week. This would be the first day that allowed time to try and reestablish regular activities. Even train service had changed as emergency crews and extra equipment were rushed up from Arlee to take over while the regular crews and locomotives were involved in the fire fighting.

*　　*　　*

The afternoon sky was increasingly dark as fluffy clouds rolled in on top of each other boiling up into billowy mountains. An occasional shadow drifted across the landscape as these mountains rolled across the face of the sun. The boys strolled lazily past the livery barn toward the railroad crossing into the company yard facility. Puffs of dry dust rose with each footfall and drifted away in the light breeze. Brett and Adam crossed the rails of the company main. To their right were the engine facility and service tracks. To their left were the storage and car maintenance tracks.

The charred remains of the logging train stood on the main storage track. It swarmed with activity as a score of workmen stripped down the flatcars to their under frames and wheel bases. Another dozen workers were busy stripping down the caboose. Crews were stripping loose debris from the locomotive as it was prepared to be towed to the engine service shop in Arlee for repair and restoration. In the engine service area, crews were busy refueling and watering engines number Thirty-Four and Forty-Six, up from the Arlee yard for temporary assignment. Both locomotives had the wide balloon stacks of the regularly operated engines, but burned coal rather than wood. Arlee had a large coal dock to service its engines. While on assignment to Snow Shoe they had been burning wood. Number Thirty-Four had large plain lettering on its tender while the lettering on number Forty-Six had an extra framing design surrounding the lettering in a yellow gold color. Both, having been used mostly for yard and freight service, were as dirty and weathered as the equipment everyone around Snow Shoe was used to.

As the boys turned their attention to the work crews and activity in the maintenance area, the two engines steamed out to work at the backlog of local freight traffic. Mr. Jackson climbed down from the frame of the caboose as he saw the boys approaching.

"Hi, Adam, Brett. What da ya hear from Bob and Stewart?" The man brushed the back of his hand across his forehead intercepting annoying beads of perspiration.

"We stopped in at the Railroad Hotel to say 'Hi' on our way over," Adam said. "They were havin' late dinner. Mr. Leary said they'd be over tomorrow ta take charge of freight operations."

"How much more has ta be done ta fix the train?" Brett asked.

"Plenty," Mr. Jackson replied. "But if we could keep at it with crews like this, we'd be done in three days easy. The "Scott" will have to be sent to Arlee's engine shop for a complete overhaul and restoration."

"Any idea how the fire started?" Adam asked.

"In all likelihood, with the high temperatures and dry conditions, it could have been spontaneous combustion in some dense underbrush," Mr. Jackson surmised.

The ten cars had been stripped down to their frames and were already under reconstruction. Some blackened timber remained on the log flats, mixed with new boards from the mill yard. The beds of the cars would be completed by the end of the day. The hardware for the side stake holders and braking system would be done tomorrow. The framing for the caboose body was under way. Most of the damaged material on the engine had been removed and it was nearly ready for number 34 to tow it down to the shop in Arlee.

Brett and Adam meandered down the line inspecting the work and looking over some of the scraps thrown to the ground. They paused at the caboose to look through the large collection of debris scattered beside the tracks. Brett kicked at the burned remains of bunks, stove, and assorted pieces. The coffeepot emerged from the pile. He squatted down and brushed through carefully with his hands, checking to see what else he might find. A tin cup fell out of a charred blanket. Brett stood up with pot and cup in hand. He turned them over in his hands, then offered them to Adam.

"These might make a good addition to your collection," Brett suggested.

"Thanks." Adam took them. "They'll have quite a special meaning. Hey, let's get the whistle cord if it's still around."

The two hurried on to the engine and checked through the discarded items on the ground. No luck.

"Mr. Wetherby," Adam called to the trainman who was cleaning window glass from the cab. "Do ya know what happened to the old whistle cord?"

"What's left of it is layin' here on the floor," Mr. Wetherby responded.

"Can I have it?"

"Help yerself." He finished picking out the last pieces of glass.

Adam and Brett climbed up into the cab. It smelled of burned wood and smoke. The older boy retrieved the cord from the floor. They stayed a short time to look over the cleanup. The fire damaged cab structure had been stripped out leaving an exposed back-head with little else but the raised seat areas for the engine crew.

"Gee, I didn't know the "Scott" had so much damage," Brett commented.

"It's a wonder, now that we're preparing it to go to the shops, that we made it at all," Mr. Wetherby added.

"Where's Jay?" Brett asked.

"They've taken the fire train inta the engine house ta repair some fittings in the pumps and hoses."

"See ya later." The boys left toward the engine house.

The wooden two-stall structure stood across from the maintenance tracks. Two tracks entered from the yard. One ended inside the facility, the other passed through a pair of doors out the rear. The front doors stood open and the boys could see the fire train within. Engine Twenty-One was visible through the rear doors, setting on the tracks outside and coupled to the end of the fire train. Jay and Scot stood near the end of a workbench, the first with his pipe in hand and the second with a cup of coffee. The boys entered by way of the tracks.

"Hi, boys," Scot and Jay greeted.

"Hi," the two responded in unison.

"Jest wanted ta see if ya were takin' the mornin' run ta Arlee," Brett said stepping up to the floor. He walked over to the tank car and leaned against the end steps.

"Sure am," Jay answered. "We'll be returnin' ta regular schedules tomorrow, sendin' number 34 back ta Arlee towing the "Scott" to the shops there and keeping number 46 here ta replace Leary's crew. As I recall, your Pa said tomorrow's trip is special."

"My ma's supposed ta be on the train. She said in her letter that she was comin' up from Baltimore and should get in on Friday." Brett reached up over his head for a grab iron and pulled himself up from the floor until he could hook his heel on the bottom step.

Adam had been showing his new treasures to Scot. Scot set his coffee cup on the workbench to inspect the discarded pot.

"Hey, Jay," he called. "Look what Adam's addin' ta his collection."

The engineer looked and smiled. "One o' these days you'll need the caboose ta store yer collection in." They all chuckled. "You boys want a ride back ta Main Street? We gotta put this train in storage and get everythin' lined up fer tomorrow's mornin' run."

"Thanks," Adam agreed.

"Can we ride the tanker?" Brett asked.

"Yea. Matt will be up with ya. Do as he says."

The boys climbed up to the board walkway and held onto the handrail. The two men turned back toward the engine. In a short time Matt Kelton climbed up from the opposite side. He positioned himself at the front to handle switching and instructed the boys to stay close to him and to hang on tightly. The whistle announced the move and the bell began its rhythmic ringing as the train moved out of the building.

The sky had darkened as the thunderheads rolled up into mountainous heaps in the sky. Passing the yard switch, the train moved into the station area where the engine would separate and run around to the other end so as to be in position to push the train onto a storage track. Thunder began to rumble in the distance. The boys rode the engine back through the yard as it turned on the wye and backed out onto the main, west of the station. Jay paused on his way across Main Street to allow the boys to disembark. Distant lightning streaked the horizon. Adam and Brett stood and watched as Twenty-One proceeded east to the switch that would cross over to the work track on the south side of the station. The engine backed across and coupled to the end of the fire train. Light rain began to fall as the train moved back toward the yard. Brett and Adam sprinted across the tracks and up Main Street toward home. After a five-minute drizzle, the storm rushed in and the flashing lightning and crashing thunder were quickly joined by a deluge of rain. The storm passed quickly, cleansing the air as twilight began to fade and the night sky crept in.

*   *   *

Brett and Adam had started for the hall stairs when Brett paused. "You go on up, Adam," he said. "I'm goin' outside a bit ta tell Pa good night."

"Okay, Little Brother. See ya shortly." Adam continued to mount the steps. Brett turned down the hall toward the kitchen.

The boy opened the screen door quietly and eased it closed after passing out to the porch. His father stood at the railing by the steps, gazing pensively at the twinkling stars. The quartering moon cast a dim light on a rain-sparkling landscape. The farm buildings were dimly visible in the shadowy light. The dark shape of the mountain loomed beyond.

Brett slipped close to his father's side. Mr. Tompkins slid his hand across his shoulders and pulled him in front of his body. The boy leaned back against the strong security of his father's presence.

"Pa, it's so beautiful up here," Brett said.

"I know, son. I love it. And I love sharing it with you."

"Do ya think Ma will like it, too?"

The man hugged his son closer. "I hope so."

"I'm glad she's comin'." The boy put his hands on his father's.

"Maybe she'll learn to like it here." He tilted his head back to look at his father's face. "Maybe we can move up here ta stay."

Mr. Tompkins glanced down to his son's eyes and smiled. "I didn't know you liked it that well."

Brett turned around and hugged his father around the waist. "I love it. Pa. I never liked a time so much as this summer."

Mr. Tompkins embraced his son and held him close. Brett reached around his father's neck and squeezed affectionately. He lay his head contentedly on his father's shoulder.

"I love you, Pa. Would you walk with me and tuck me in ta bed?"

"Sure, son. Let's go."

Mr. Tompkins turned to the door with this son at his side. Brett reached out and pulled the door open. The door slammed shut behind them.

* * *

The countryside lay bathed in the bright morning sun. Green forested slopes stretched along the landscape. A plume of black smoke advanced through the trees. Rounding a bend, the train burst into view, paused to pick up the morning track walker, rattled across the Chamber's Crossing, and continued on its way to Snow Shoe. A coach, a mixed, and a baggage made up the regular Friday train from Arlee. Mrs. Tompkins sat near the aisle in the front of the coach. Her long brown hair was brushed smooth, rolled up, and secured in place with small ivory combs. Her dainty countenance was lit by a smile as she spoke with Dan Seegers and learned of the recent events in the lives of her husband and son. Dan sat across the aisle with his back toward the end of the coach.

"I've enjoyed hearing all you've told me of Teddy and Brett. It hardly seems Brett could have done and learned so much in these past two months."

"Ma'am, Brett's a wonderful boy and it's pleasured me greatly to see the joy with which he does things."

"You really think he's enjoyed being in the back country?"

"Oh, definitely. He's a very happy boy."

"Well, sir, I've come to sense that in his letters and decided to see what it is that gives him such fun and excitement."

"I do hope you'll decide to stay awhile." The conductor rose to his feet. "Mr. Tompkins has been good for the company. Perhaps you might even consider moving up here as a family."

Her smile faded slightly. "That's a bit presumptuous, Mr. Seegers. I've not even considered the possibility."

"I wish you an enjoyable visit, Mrs. Tompkins. We're almost there. Please excuse me."

"Thank you for your kind conversation." She smiled once more. The conductor turned to the door and was gone.

* * *

Brett and his father and Adam paused at the corner of Main and Railroad. The morning activity of the town was alive and strong. Several wagons were en route to their various destinations as pedestrians scurried busily about.

"See you folks later," Adam said. "Ya have a good day. Brett, you tell your ma I said 'Hi' and hope she had a good trip."

"You bet, Adam. Maybe we'll stop by the Herald later." Brett watched as his friend started up the wooden walk.

"Have a good day, Adam," Mr. Tompkins waved.

The two of them waited for traffic to clear, then started across the street. They crossed the two tracks on the south side of the station. The end of the platform was busy with the activity of people gathering to meet the train. Mr. Tompkins and his son crossed the wooden platform to the station. They would check briefly to see if the train was expected on time. They were soon back out on the platform having been informed that the train was on schedule.

Brett walked out to the track and looked toward the bend for signs of smoke. The track remained empty; the air remained clear. There was no distant sound to indicate that the train was near. Mr. Tompkins walked to the edge of the platform roof and leaned against a post.

"Pa," Brett spoke from where he stood between the rails. "I'm all excited inside." He looked toward his father and jammed his hands into his pockets. "I can't wait for the train."

Mr. Tompkins stood up and walked out to his son. He laid a hand across Brett's shoulder. "I know, son. I'm kind a jumpy inside myself. Don't think I can stand still. Why don't we sit down and wait. We're early yet."

The man and his son strolled over to a bench and sat down. Mr. Tompkins put his hands behind his head and stretched back. Brett sat at the edge of the seat watching down the track.

"I'm gonna walk some."

The boy got up and wandered across the platform toward the siding switch. He paused at the switch, then walked along the station platform balancing himself on a rail. He reached the end of the platform at Main Street, then headed back to the bench where his father had been. But Mr. Tompkins had walked back to lean against the post and watch. Brett joined him there. He stood in front of his father a moment.

Then, leaning back, he warned, "Catch me, Pa."

The man reached out and hooked the falling form under the arms with his hands. He pulled his son back against him and laid his hands across his son's chest. There they waited.

Minutes passed. Suddenly Brett tensed and turned his head to listen. "Hear something?" his father asked.

"I think so." The boy paused. "Yes!" He stared at the treetops. Then he pointed. "There she is! See the smoke?"

His father followed his outstretched hand and studied the trees. "I see it, too!" he announced.

The drifting smoke drew closer. It stopped and rose in a straight black column.

"She's at the switch," Brett explained.

It seemed to slide forward, then stopped again. After a brief pause it again advanced toward them. The whistle sounded – two long wailing calls, a short blast, then a final scream which hung on the air and echoed back from the mountains. The column approached the bend. Suddenly the train was in full view drawing rapidly closer to the station.

Brett swung around to face his father, then grabbing both hands pulled him joyously toward the open platform.

"She's come, Pa! She's really come!" The boy's face was aglow with excitement.

The two of them walked quickly out onto the open platform as the engine slowed. Steam burst from the pistons and the black smoke boiled from the stack. Air blasted through the brakes setting metal screeching against metal. The engine passed with bell ringing. Scot waved a greeting which Brett returned, and nodded in answer to the unasked question. Brett leaned beside his father with an arm slipped around the man's waist. The cars glided to a halt as air and steam blasted through hoses and cylinders. Dan Seegers stepped out from the coach followed by several passengers. He descended to the station area and placed a stool at the bottom of the steps. Passengers began to disembark. Mrs. Tompkins stepped out to the platform.

"Ma!" Brett called. He jumped up and down and waved excitedly. "Ma! Over here!"

She waved. Mr. Tompkins and his son rushed to meet her. She had barely reached the wooden platform when her son rushed into her arms.

"Oh, Ma! I'm so glad you're here!" He hugged her and kissed her, then gave his father a turn.

She beamed with joy and hugged and kissed them both. "Brett, Teddy, I've missed you both so much." Tears of joy slid down her cheeks.

"Come," said Mr. Tompkins. "Let's get your things. We've so much to tell you and to show you."

"I'll get them." Brett rushed off to the baggage wagon. Jarrett helped him get the traveling bags down. There were four of them.

"Leave them, son. We'll ask Adam to pick them up when he brings the papers over."

The three of them turned toward the street at the end of the station area. Brett put his hand in his mother's and skipped along beside her. At the street she took her husband's arm and they turned toward the Tylers' home. Brett walked along just ahead so he could point out landmarks as they went.

The train stood quietly alongside the station, waiting to move on toward Day's End. Steam hissed from the pistons and thumped softly in its belly. The boy, his father, and his mother disappeared into the crowd headed away from the station.

It was a radiantly sunny morning on the first day of August.

A Gathering

A SEQUEL TO
Summer at Stewart Creek

A GATHERING

The sharp ring of the ax cut through the silence of the falling snow. Broken pieces of wood clattered to the hard frozen ground. Another chunk was stood upon the stump. The man lifted the ax high, brought it down hard, and split the wood chunk easily.

"Son," he spoke to the boy standing nearby, "take this load in ta yer ma. See what ya kin do ta help inside. I'll finish up here and bring in the last load."

"Sure, Pa." He gathered the pieces and turned toward the back porch with arms loaded.

Silent snow padded the upper surfaces of fence boards, tree limbs, wood chunks, and intricate branchwork of shrubs. Soft dry powder muffled the boy's footfalls, so he seemed to glide ghostlike through the falling white atmosphere toward the squares of light that marked the warm kitchen of the large structure. The yellow wooden hotel building, trimmed in green, stood nestled between the tracks, across the street from Arlee's station building. Jason climbed the porch steps and entered the warm fragrance of the Railroad Hotel's kitchen.

Dropping the wood into its holding box near the range, the eleven-year-old unbundled himself and hung his coat and hat on their pegs beside the back door. His wet gloves and scarf were draped over the wooden bars which reached out from the wall behind the large black wood-burning range. Mrs. Johnston set a pair of cookie trays into the oven, then turned to the work table to shovel a fresh batch of Christmas tree sugar cookies onto the cooling cloths.

"Is your pa on his way in?" she asked.

Jason stood by the stove rubbing the snow from his light brown hair, then holding his hands toward the warmth to dry them.

"He'll be along soon's he finishes the last load. How long 'til the trains come in?"

"'Bout an hour yet. There're some fresh greens in the bucket near the stairs. Why don't ya add them around in the dining room and check the fires."

"Okay, Ma."

The Johnstons owned and operated the Railroad Hotel at Arlee, West Virginia. Arlee was the center of the Virginia and Truckee Railroad operations. All trains stopped at the station, just across the street, which also housed the central offices. The main yards and shops were at the southern end of town. The tracks ran down both sides of the station to handle transfer traffic northbound and southbound and from the branches to Snow Shoe and Summit.

The door opened and Mr. Johnston stomped in with an armload of wood. He dropped it onto the heap overflowing from the box.

"How's dinner comin'?" The tall sturdy man hung his hat and coat on their pegs and walked toward the stove with gloves and scarf in hand. "Sure smells good." He reached up and added the wet items to the collection on the wooden arms.

"The roast is brownin'," his wife informed. Her slight body moved with light quickness of long practice as she checked the sheet of cookies, the roast, and the pots on the top of the hot metal. "It'll all come done in an hour. You an Jason best clean up. Ya kin meet the trains. When yer back it'll be time enough ta lay the table."

"Where's Jason?"

"Checkin' the fires."

He kissed her lightly on the cheek. "See ya after a bit." The man left the room.

*   *   *

Steam drifted past the outside of the frosted coach windows. Noisily people bustled along the aisle seeking seats or making their way toward the doors. The boy and his mother talked excitedly in their seat, glancing at the activity on the station platform outside their window or at the movement within. Slowly the commotion settled. Outside a voice called, "All aboard!", a whistle screeched back with two sharp blasts, and the station began to slip away with the clattering motion of the car.

Ludington passed from view and the window light reflected off a wall of drifting white flakes, swirling in the draft wash of the moving train.

The whistle cut through the twilight several times as the string of lighted windows was drawn steadily along the tracks.

Mrs. Tompkins' warming happiness was the best Christmas gift her son could want. For more that a year her husband, Brett's father, had been away working a logging company in the mountain country around Snow Shoe. His mother's dainty beauty had been overshadowed by her discontent with Teddy's new interest in a family business from which he'd long been detached. The life of a banker's wife in Baltimore was far more secure and comfortable than the rough existence in a logging town.

But last summer had set the stage for a new look at things. Brett had spent the summer with his father and his enthusiasm and joy for life in Snow Shoe had given cause to reconsider. So after a sudden decision to visit last August, Eli had agreed to allow her husband another year with the Stewart Creek Logging Company and to make several visits with their son. Unlike last Christmas's separation, they decided to gather with friends and family for a Christmas sharing this season.

The friendship with the Johnston family stretched over three generations. Jason was one of the first friends Brett had made last summer. Their grandfathers were friends some forty years back when the railroad and logging companies were just entering the mountains. Grandpa Tompkins and Teddy would arrive from Snow Shoe on tomorrow morning's train. Jason's grandmother and grandfather Laige, on his mother's side, would be arriving from Pine Bluff on this evening's southbound.

"Ma," Brett was watching the snowfall, "I think this is gonna be the best Christmas ever." He leaned back in his seat and smiled at his mother. "I've not seen you so happy in so long. And I'm gonna see Grandpa and Pa and Jason's family. I feel so good!" The boy shivered with excitement.

Eli put her arms around her eleven-year-old son and hugged him close. She rubbed her chin lightly in his tossled auburn hair and smiled at their reflection in the window glass. Brett smiled back.

"I know how you feel, Son. I, too, feel a new excitement that I haven't known for a long time." She leaned back into the softness of the coach seat with Brett nestled against her side. "This is to be a very special Christmas with special friends and family to share it."

"I'm so glad we'll get ta see everybody," Brett said. "It seems so unreal that so many people who mean so much will be comin' tomorrow."

The engine's whistle cut into the night. Lights approached and began to flash by. They were passing the engine facility. The train slowed. Rail yards slipped by. The edge of Arlee slid slowly by as the train approached the station. Brakes squealed. Air hissed through the lines. The car shuddered and clattered to a halt.

Brett and his mother gazed through the window and the silent snowfall beyond to the people gathered in the lamplight on the station platform. The motion attracted their attention and they waved back eagerly to Jason and his father. Quickly, Mrs. Tompkins and her son reached down their bags and turned toward the platform door.

Jason and his father met them as they stepped from the coach steps. Steam hissed from the hose connections under the open platforms and misted into the falling snow. The station hummed with conversation and activity. Shouts, embraces, laughter, rattling baggage wagon wheels, grating trunks, clattering footfalls, filled the air with the noise of Christmas gatherings.

Some of the crowd had drifted away toward town. A distant whistle echoed off the hillsides north of town. The southbound from Pine Bluff was approaching.

"That's Grandma and Grandpa Laige's train!" Jason announced excitedly.

Quickly the four dashed around the station building to the track on the other side. The glow of the headlamp floated in the snow dust far up the track. It grew larger then swung straight at them as the locomotive rounded the bend. The bell began its rhythmic ringing as the whistle announced the train's arrival. The engine churned past the small group waiting on the platform, hissing steam and billowing smoke as it slowed. Brakes screeched and clattered as the train rumbled to a stop.

The chaos of new arrivals began again after a very brief quiet. In the middle of the commotion, Jason's grandparents disembarked from their car and the six of them slipped away, across the street to the hotel.

Franklin and Martha Laige were in their early 60's, living in retirement in Pine Bluff where they shared a small cottage and enjoyed lazy days of gardening and time with friends. Nearly a dozen years had passed since they turned the hotel business over to their son-in-law and daughter.

Entering the lobby was like entering a new chaos all over again as new arrivals registered to spend the night. A few would stay for the holidays, but most would leave again in the morning to continue their private journeys, each to his own gathering.

Hank Johnston and his son stayed to help check in the new guests. Brett led his mother and Jason's grandparents to the kitchen to await the family.

*   *   *

Dinner that evening was a festive gathering with the various guests sharing news from their various points of origin and the stories of their travels. Following dinner the Johnston and Tompkins families brought each other up to date as they shared in the duties of cleaning up the dinner dishes. Adjourning to the parlor they brought in packages and placed them under the tree. The boys played at dominoes while their elders continued to visit, and shared with each other the events of their separate lives since departing for school in September.

Brett shared Jason's room as he had during previous visits. They listened to the night sounds of activity in the rail yard. The steady silent swish of the soft snowfall continued outside as they drifted into slumber.

*   *   *

December twenty-fourth dawned with a brilliant radiance reflected from a wintry world of sparkling white. The bright sunlight fell across the boys where they slept. Its warmth penetrated their consciousness. Brett opened his eyes, squinted, then turned his head away from the painful brightness.

"Jason," he shook his friend, "it's mornin'. The train from Snow Shoe should be comin'."

"Huh?" Jason stirred. "It's cold!"

"Let's go! The train's comin'! My pa'll be here!"

"Oh, yeh."

The two dressed quickly in the chill air of the bedroom. Clattering down the stairs, they were still tucking in their shirt tails as they burst into the warmth of the kitchen.

"What time is it?" Jason asked.

"The train's due in forty-five minutes," his father read his mind. "I've taken the day off from the agency. Clarence is running things today. So ya take yer time, eat, and I'll tend ta things here."

"Thanks, Pa," Jason beamed. "Mornin' Grandpa and Grandma."

"Good morning, Jason," they replied. "Gonna be a mighty busy day," his grandfather commented.

"Sure is!"

"Morning', Ma," Brett greeted kissing her lightly as he ran to find a plate and settle to a place at the kitchen table.

Greetings were exchanged all around. The adults had eaten and first breakfast had been served to the guests leaving on the morning trains. Jason and Brett wolfed down their breakfasts, grabbed their coats and hats, and dashed down the hall through the lobby and out the front door.

The holiday crowd was in a jovial mood as they awaited connections so they could finish their journeys, or awaited the arrival of family or friends. Skillfully, the boys nudged their way toward the edge of the platform where they could see the train coming.

Five minutes passed. A whistle called to the south. The train from Summit was arriving. Over the next twenty minutes it came in on the outside pass track, unloaded, had its engine turned and serviced, then pulled onto the siding for its hour-long layover.

At seven-fifty, the echoing whistle of Engine Twenty-one hailed the arrival of the train from Snow Shoe. Brett was filled with excitement as he watched it approach. Memories of last summer heightened his anticipations and he stepped out to get a good view of the approaching locomotive. Jay Miller was at the throttle. Scot O'Donnell was firing.

Brett waved wildly, "Mr. Miller! Mr. O'Donnell! It's me, Brett!"

The bearded engineer recognized the boy. A broad grin lit his face. He waved. Scot stepped to the edge of the cab's platform and waved, too. Then the engineer acknowledged with a short whistle blast. Back on the coach platform, conductor Dan Seegers heard the blast and looked for the boy. Then he, too, waved. The train slowed.

"Merry Christmas, Brett!" the engine crew called as the locomotive went by.

"Merry Christmas!" Brett beamed.

Almost before the train had stopped, the conductor reached for and shook Brett's outstretched hand. Brett's father was the first to get off and swept the boy into an ecstatic embrace.

"I brought some friends, Brett. Boy, have I missed you, Son." They both beamed with joy as they squeezed each other tightly.

When Brett was again on his feet he turned to see who else had come. Grandpa Tompkins was there and shared a great bear hug. It had been more that a year since the two had seen each other. In his late 60's, he had come up from Baltimore to spend the holiday season with his son in Snow Shoe. As always, a hug from him included a brush with his neatly trimmed graying beard.

The Tylers with whom Brett had stayed the last summer exchanged greetings as they disembarked from the rail coach. "How ya doin, Brett," Adam greeted.

"Okay. How's things at the Herald? Gee I've missed ya!"

"The paper's fine. I've kinda missed you, too."

Much to Brett's surprise, Horace Leeds, the camp cook and doctor was with them. Horace limped across to the boy and reached for his outstretched hand. Brett saw a glistening in the old man's eyes and at once felt a great surge of love for his lonely friend. Tears of joyful surprise welled up in the boy's eyes. He slipped both arms around his friend's waist and squeezed tightly.

"Mr. Leeds, I sure am glad you're here." He exclaimed with the joy and love that he felt for this old friend's unexpected arrival.

"Missed ya somethin' powerful on the mountain, Boy." He, too, felt a tear escape as he held this boy whom he'd come to love and respect from the visit of the previous summer.

Mrs. Tompkins had come across when the whistle had first announced the train's coming. As she witnessed Brett's reunion of love and excitement with old friends of the past summer, she felt a tenseness of emotion grip her from within, and a dampness glistening cold and moist on her cheek. In her heart she wept with joy, for she knew now that her gift this Christmas was a precious one indeed.

The woman embraced her husband and renewed her acquaintance with the Tylers. Adam joined with Brett and Jason and the three boys excused themselves. Horace stood alone a moment.

"Get your things and join us in the kitchen. Won't you, Mr. Leeds," Eli invited. "I never got to the mountain on my visit, and would greatly appreciate it if you'd tell me about life up there."

The white-haired man smiled. "I'd like that fine, M'am."

"We'll see you all for dinner tonight," Mr. Tompkins waved to the conductor.

"Wouldn't miss it for the world!" the man exclaimed.

The reunited group of family and friends fell into small knots of conversation as they drifted away toward the hotel.

*   *   *

As the day eased its course toward evening, all were busy with preparations for dinner and for an evening gathering in celebration of Christmas, but more significantly, in celebration of life. It was a gathering of family and friends to unite the past with the present and the present with the future. Grandpa Tompkins hadn't seen the Laiges for years. The memories of an age long past were recalled in a day of checkers, hot coffee, Christmas cookies, and reflections. Eli and Teddy brought each other up to date with each other's doings since summer. Horace shared his view of logging life on the mountain, then fell into reminiscing about the time Brett had spent at the camp. The Tylers and the Johnstons got in on the news sharing as well, along with Grandpa Tompkins and the Laiges. All spent the day in the kitchen working on the dinner and sharing experiences and friendship. The three boys were in and out, mostly out, playing in the snow and sampling the fresh baked goods with hot chocolate for inner warmth.

The afternoon slipped away. Fading sunlight played out shadows across a snow-scaped yard torn apart with playful snowball fights and chases and the labor of constructing a snowman. Widening swaths marked paths where the snow boulders were created to make the figure which stood silhouetted against the rich reds and blues of the sunset sky.

The kitchen door burst open and the warmth exploded with boisterous chatter and the clomping of snow-crusted boots and a sharp draft of cold, cut off as the door banged shut again.

"You boys have a good time?" Jason's mother asked as she spooned the drippings over a turkey.

"Yeh," the boys chorused.

"Don't track that snow all about," Mrs. Johnston admonished. "Next thing ya know we'll all be pushin' mops." She smiled as she slipped the turkey back into the oven.

"Why don't you bring in tonight's firewood while you're still bundled up," Mr. Tompkins suggested.

"You boys bring it ta the porch an we'll take it from there," Mr. Tyler added. "We can put up enough for tamorra' as well and save Christmas Day fer doin' things without worryin' on chores."

"Sounds good," Jason replied.

"Let's go to it." Adam turned to the door.

The wood boxes were filled to overflowing with extra pieces stacked beside. Wet clothes were hung behind the stove and the boys retreated to Jason's room to change into dry apparel. They returned to the kitchen in time to help move the serving dishes to the long table in the dining room.

Since family and friends occupied most of the hotel's rooms, there would be few guests to dinner. The de Philemon family was staying over. Spending the day visiting friends, they would return for dinner, then be gone again Christmas Day with relatives.

Jason returned to the kitchen. "Ma," he asked, "how come there's extra places set? Outside of the folks in room five, I count three more plates."

Mrs. Johnston stirred the gravy bubbling in the large frying pan. The clock on the mantle in the sitting room struck five. "We still have three guests comin'. Sort of a surprise. Should be here shortly."

"Who?" Jason questioned.

A distant whistle echoed joyfully in the hills.

"Mr. Miller and Mr. O'Donnell and Mr. Seegers," he answered his own question.

Brett dashed into the kitchen. "Ain't that Twenty-one's whistle?!" he asked excitedly.

"Sure is," Jason replied.

Mrs. Johnston smiled. "Thought ya might enjoy some other guests fer dinner. Seems we've already gathered so many, what's three more."

"You bet!" Brett exclaimed.

There was a brief explosion of activity as the boys ran out to the station to meet the train, final preparations were made for dinner, and everyone gathered around the table.

*   *   *

The hotel's dining room stretched the length of the hall from the lobby to the kitchen with a single table, long enough and wide enough to seat twenty people comfortably. A fireplace on the side wall between two windows warmed the room. The table was spread with a dinner of turkey, stuffing, cranberry, potatoes, corn, beans, biscuits, fruit breads, assorted relishes, and baked goods. All had gathered and were enjoying the story of how the Johnstons and the Tompkins had decided to get everyone together for this Christmas gathering.

"Please pass a biscuit, Mr. Laige," Brett asked.

"Sure, Son. Catch!" He tossed it half the length of the table to the boy on the other side.

"Franklin!" his wife chastised.

Brett caught the biscuit. "Nice throw." His mother shot a disapproving glance.

"Why, Mother," Mrs. Johnston reflected, "that reminds me of the time when I was a girl and we were gathered to dinner on the farm durin' hayin' season."

"Yes, and yer pa helped hisself ta the gravy, with all the flies buzzin' around; then held it while they landed, and stirred em all in afore passin' it on."

"You did that?!" Jason laughed.

"Yup," his grandfather smiled.

Everyone laughed heartily at the reflection.

Brett had buttered his biscuit and taken a bite. He chewed thoughtfully.

"Hey! I know these biscuits. I'd know them anywhere!" He looked toward Horace who ignored the stare, though not for long.

He smiled, "Ya don't 'spect me ta spend a whole day in a kitchen an not do nothin'."

"Guess not. I've sort a missed em, too. I never could make em good as you."

*   *   *

Following dinner and a mass cleanup operation, everyone adjourned to the sitting room. Wood was added to the fire until it leaped merrily spreading light and warmth into the room. A tree decorated with small fruits and nuts and paper cuttings strung on shining red ribbons, and strings of popcorn, stood in the corner near the window. A number of packages had been stowed beneath. Bright wrappings invited curious handling. Mixed in with the large packages were several small ones -- wishing gifts, Brett's mother called them. They were special for Christmas Eve.

Grandpa Tompkins officiated with the assistance of Grandpa Laige, and with great ceremony these little packages were distributed. Mr. Johnston smiled when he found a smoothly whittled letter opener tucked carefully into folded paper within his small package. Mrs. Tyler opened a package containing fragile laced handkerchiefs. Jay Miller's package contained a tightly folded red bandanna. A small, brightly wrapped box was labeled "for Brett and his father."

"I wonder what it can be," Teddy thought aloud.

"We hafta share it," Brett observed.

"You open it," his father offered.

Carefully Brett untied the ribbon and unwrapped the package. He lifted the lid on a small white box. Inside was a carefully folded piece of paper. Brett handed it to his father. It rustled as Mr. Tompkins unfolded it and everyone else waited in silent anticipation of its contents.

Teddy began to read:

To my dearest son, Brett, and my dearest husband, Teddy,

I love you more than anything else in this world. Your happiness is my happiness; your sadness, my sadness; your joy, my joy. I have watched each of you these past months and have seen happiness and joy which you have longed for me to share in some dark uncivilized corner of the back country. I've known the sadness of separation and of Brett's homesickness after he returned from last summer's visit. I've come to meet the people of the world you love and find myself happy in their company. It is with anticipated excitement and adventure that I have decided we should all share this new life together. I may even find that it's not so uncivilized after all.

*A very special Merry Christmas
with all my love,*

Mother

His voice cracked hoarsely as he finished reading. Tears ran down his cheeks and dropped quietly onto his shirt. Brett's eyes blurred with happiness as he crawled to where his mother sat with her back against the chair Grandpa occupied.

"Ma," he cried softly, "I love you. I love you."

His father folded the paper tenderly and put it back in its box. He looked at his wife.

"Honey, thank you. There's never been a more precious gift than what you've just given to us."

"Merry Christmas," Grandpa Tompkins added softly.

The words echoed quietly around the room growing louder as the joy everyone felt swelled until it filled the gathering.

"Merry Christmas!"

BACK ALBUM

Summer at Stewart Creek takes place along the fictitious Virginia and Truckee Railroad of West Virginia, a map of which is reproduced in the front of the book. The V&TRR is reproduced in miniature by the author. Photography from the model railroad is used in the photographic material within the book. Following is a photo album taken from photo shoots taken to select the photographs used within the story. The story begins in Arlee where Brett meets Jason on his first night along the V&T. This photo shoot was of Arlee station, the hotel, and engine #21.

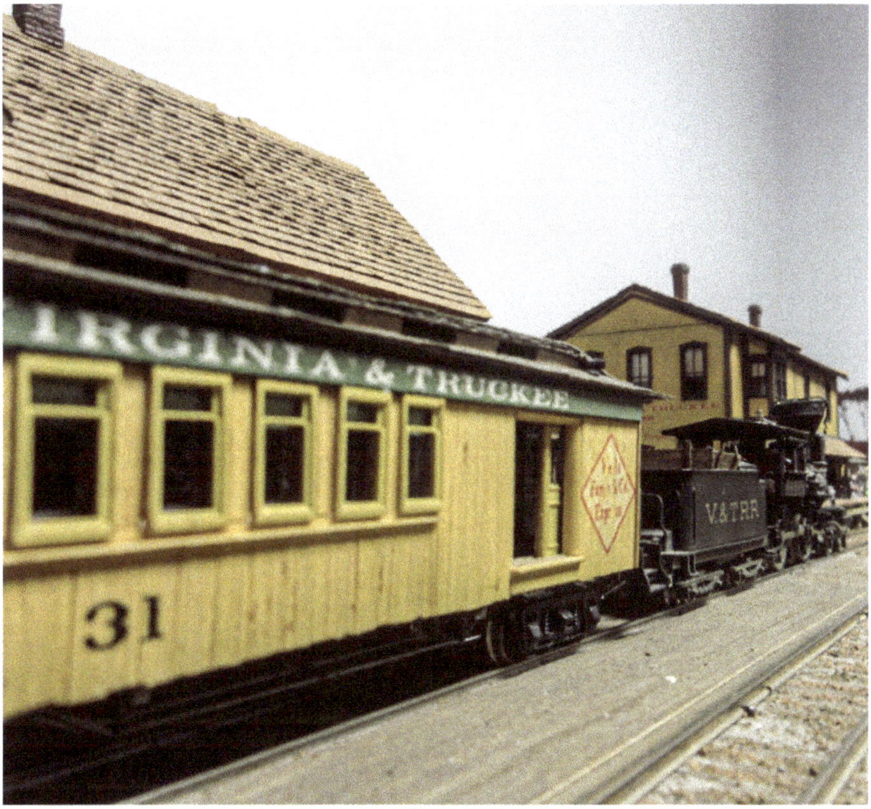
IRGINIA & TRUCKEE
31
V&TRR

V&TRR

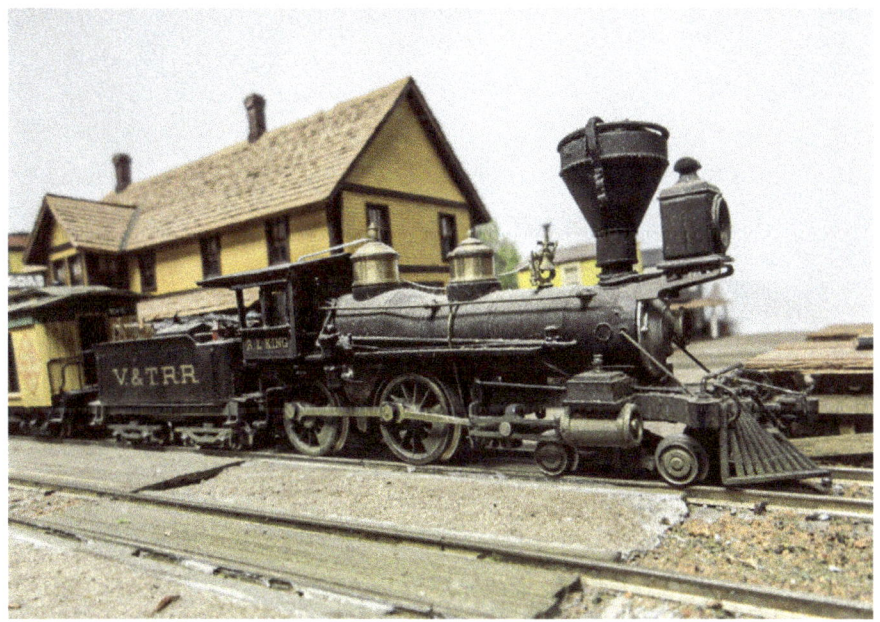

The Stewart Creek Logging Company is located in Snow Shoe where its primary locomotive is the "Scott" #2 and #21 the "R L King" is home based as the service locomotive for the Snow Shoe branch out of Arlee. Following are photographs from Snow Shoe, the logging company's engine facility, and the two locomotives.

Brett's trip from Baltimore to Snow Shoe required a transfer from the Baltimore and Ohio Railroad to the Virginia and Truckee Railroad at the junction at Truckee, West Virginia. This is a look at Truckee station and engine facility.

The Station at Day's End

The Station at Blakesville

After the "Scott's" damaging trip through the forest fire on the mountain in the chapter "Ordeal by Fire," the damaged locomotive was taken to the shops at Arlee for repair and restoration. Here's a look at the locomotive in the shops.

The engine facilities at Arlee were the primary engine storage and service facilities for the Virginia and Truckee Railroad.

Two locomotives were sent to Snow Shoe to help handle the traffic while the "Scott" was out of service. "Kidner" #34 and "Kidd" #46 moved from service out of Truckee to service on the Snow Shoe branch. Here they are in Truckee.

Finally, here are a scattering of photos at different locations of life after dark.

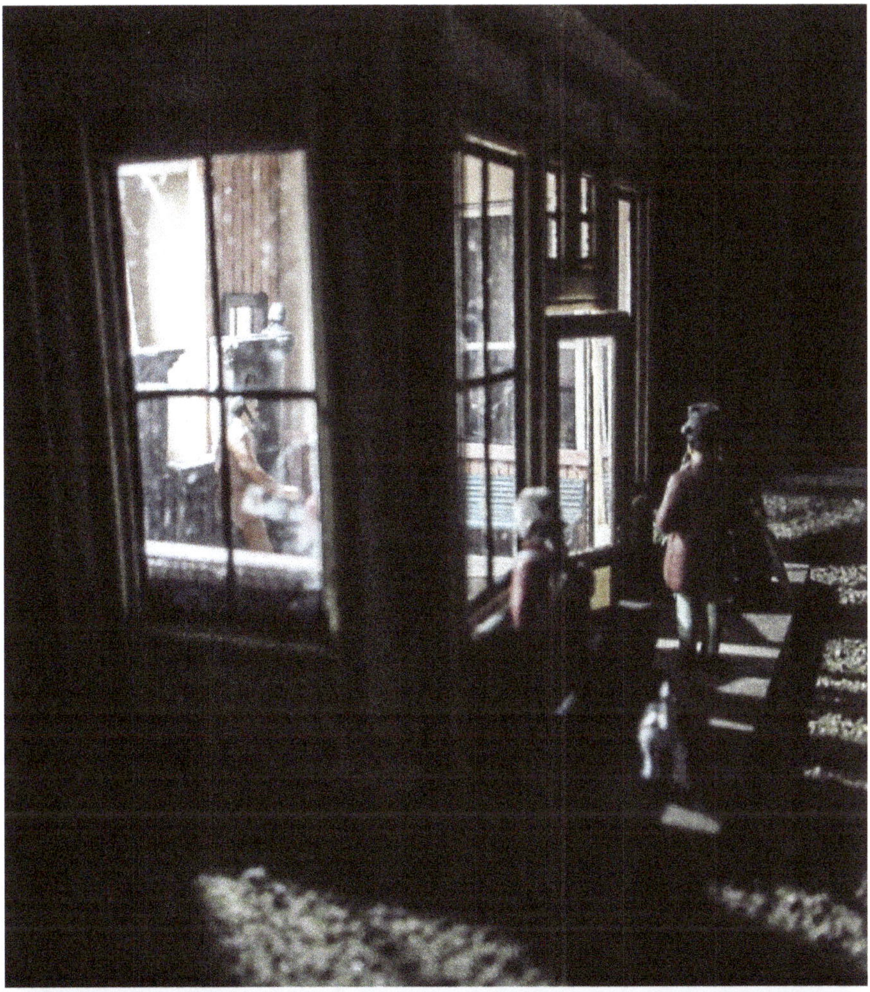

GLASS
HARDWARE AND STEAM FITTINGS.

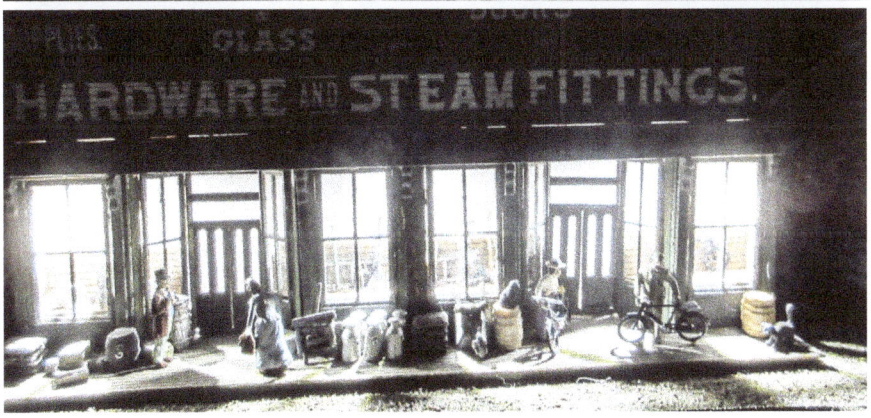

THE BOYS BEHIND THE STORY

The author spent the summer of 1979 as a counselor at Camp Good News on Cape Cod, Massachusetts. These three campers became the inspiration for a story in remembrance of that summer. Written during the winter of 1979-80, Summer at Stewart Creek has remained in manuscript form these many decades. The original manuscript books contained pencil drawings of these three in the front. The author hadn't taken any character shots. These photos were taken at the camp that summer.

Brett Thomas, in the story as Brett Tompkins, is standing by the tent pole in the author's tent. Jason Jones, in the story as Jason Johnston, is sitting on the trunk.

Adam Thomas, in the story as Adam Tyler, is in the center, in period dress for the 4th of July parade and events of 1979.

ABOUT THE AUTHOR
J. ARTHUR MOORE

J. Arthur Moore is an educator with 42 years experience in public, private, and independent settings. He is also an amateur photographer and has illustrated his works with his own photographs. In addition to **Summer at Stewart Creek** Mr. Moore has written **Journey into Darkness**, a story in four parts, **Blake's Story, Revenge and Forgiveness**, two Civil War historic fictions, **Summer of Two Worlds**, a Native American historic fiction set in Montana Territory in the summer of 1882. He recently published a third Civil War era historic fiction, **West to Freedom**. This latest work is pure fiction, set in the fictitious territory of his Virginia and Truckee Railroad of West Virginia, which he has recreated in miniature and used to illustrate this story.

A graduate of Jenkintown High School, just outside of Philadelphia, Pennsylvania, Moore attended West Chester State College, currently West Chester University. Upon graduation, he joined the Navy and was stationed in Norfolk, Virginia, where he met his wife to be, a widow with four children. Once discharged from the service, he moved to Coatesville,

Pennsylvania, began his teaching career, married and brought his new family to live in a 300-year-old farm house in which the children grew up and married, went their own ways, raised their families to become grandparents themselves.

Retiring after a 42-year career, Mr. Moore has moved to the farming country in Lancaster County, Pennsylvania, where he plans to enjoy the generations of family, time with his model railroad, and time to guide his writings into a new life through publication. It also allows for the opportunity to participate in a local model railroad club as well as time for traveling to Civil War events, and presenting at various organizations and events about the boys who were part of that war. He also shares the process of writing, and readings from his work, and does book signings at a variety of locations.

Mr. Moore can be reached through the contact page of the website for his books at www.jarthurmoore.com with links to his Facebook and Twitter pages; and a boys page focusing on the stories of the boys who served in the Civil War.

www.ingramcontent.com/pod-product-compliance
Lightning Source LLC
Chambersburg PA
CBHW040017250626
47171CB00006B/34